ABOUT THIS BOOK

Welcome to Havenwood Falls, a small town in the majestic mountains of Colorado. A town where legacies began centuries ago, bloodlines run deep, and dark secrets abound. A town where nobody is what you think, where truths pose as lies, and where myths blend with reality. A place where everyone has a story. Including the high schoolers. This is only but one...

The Kasun wolf pack has always been led by a female alpha, but when Willa Kasun's mother died to give her life, her father stepped in as leader. Now that she's about to come of age, the pack will once again be led by a female, as it is meant to be. Except Willa hasn't shifted yet.

Less wolf and more cub-dud, Willa has until her next birthday to shift and claim her place as alpha, or she'll lose it forever—something her pack mates won't let her forget. The few supernatural powers that have manifested are her secret and the only hope she has of unleashing her wolf.

Distractions of life as a junior at Havenwood Falls High provide a escape from the pack's pressure, making Willa feel more like a teenager and less like an alpha every day. Then there's Tarron Wilde, a sarcastic and striking elf, who makes her wonder if being alpha is really what she wants.

Her heart yearns for a reality unfamiliar and feared by her pack, while her mind can't accept being replaced as alpha. The future of her entire pack relies on Willa's choice—embrace what was written in the stars so long ago or choose to fight for what her heart desires.

WRITTEN IN THE STARS

A HAVENWOOD FALLS HIGH NOVELLA

KALLIE ROSS

HAVENWOOD FALLS HIGH BOOKS

Written in the Stars by Kallie Ross

Reawakened by Morgan Wylie

The Fall by Kristen Yard

Somewhere Within by Amy Hale

Awaken the Soul by Michele G. Miller

Bound by Shadows by Cameo Renae

Fata Morgana by E.J. Fechenda

Forever Emeline by Katie M. John

Reclamation by AnnaLisa Grant

Avenoir by Daniele Lanzarotta

Avenge the Heart by Michele G. Miller

Curse the Night by R.K. Ryals

Blood & Iron by Amy Hale

Shadows & Spells by Cameo Renae

Falling Deep by J.L. Weil

Saving Infiniti by Rose Garcia

Willful by Liz Ferry

Cast in Moonlight by Ali Winters

Promise the Moon by Kallie Ross

Blurred Lines by Daniele Lanzarotta

Ascending Darkness by J.L. Weil

Finding Infiniti by Rose Garcia

Unicorn's Lament by Megan Linski

Paper Bird by Amy Richie

Predestined by Valia Lind

Rediscovered by Morgan Wylie

Ashes of Fate by Apryl Baker

Stay up to date at www.HavenwoodFalls.com

OTHER BOOKS BY KALLIE ROSS

Dedicated to my wolf-shifter-loving bestie, Gaby.

CHAPTER 1

On her first day back in the Havenwood Falls High lunchroom, Willa Kasun leaned on the doorframe, watching the human and paranormal students carefully shelve themselves into the right sections, as if it were a grocery store. Vampires hovered around a refrigerated soda machine in the corner that served more than cola. Most humans, unaware of the supernatural community around them, wondered why the bottom left button never worked for them, so they stopped pushing it. Elves basked in the sun at a wall of windows to the left. Shifters huddled with their kind, clustered around tables at the center of the room, where Willa's wolf-shifter pack made the most noise. And humans, well, they actually outnumbered them all.

Humans unknowingly fist-bumped shifter athletes, sipped soda with vamps, and made plans to go to the Burger Bar after school with supes. Living a normal life was the point of living in Havenwood Falls, and Willa looked forward to stepping out of the comfort of her pack and into the melting pot of high school. She wondered where she'd fit in. She wasn't human and she hadn't shifted. She belonged nowhere and everywhere.

Havenwood Falls High was the picture of diversity. Every kind, color, and race walked the halls, but pride, fear, and ignorance had a way of keeping most supernaturals with their own species. While popular teen movies about supernaturals missed the mark about much, they nailed their angsty adolescent attitudes, even with nearly half of the population in Havenwood Falls being supernatural. Their ability to shift or exert super-strength didn't make life any easier, because they hid all the messy magic stuff from the humans who walked the hallways with them.

Willa heard and felt a growl vibrating from her right, and as she glanced up, she caught the dark eyes of a brooding dragon shifter. He set his tray down as another student, an elf, scooted over for him. But, as a shifter, he should have joined the other dragons three rows back.

Willa tilted her head, confused.

The dragon—Bale, if Willa remembered correctly—made himself comfortable with a group of supernaturals who resembled the checkout lane of the grocery more than the aisles —an array of items piled together. Multiple supernatural races had convened, all courteous and reticent, and no one outside their bubble seemed to take notice. Willa certainly hadn't regarded them in years past.

"Hey, Will," Willa's brother, also named Will, short for William, called.

Willa rolled her eyes. "Hey, *li'l* Kase."

Growing up with a sheriff for a dad and no mother had Willa acting like another one of the boys in their small community, so she'd often been called "Will." To keep the confusion to a minimum, though, and because her brother was the mini-me to their father, everyone called Will "li'l Kase." Half of the nickname fell by the wayside when Kase outgrew his dad. Among the pack that lived in the woods, the Kasun twins had a reputation for being mischievous, and the nicknames helped distinguish between the two when their older brothers wanted to blame one of them for something. A few of the elders had referred to them as *the boy version* and *the girl version*.

"It's Willa at school. I don't want you giving your entourage any ideas," Willa warned her brother.

He nodded his consent. "I'll add the *a* if you subtract the *li'l*." He nudged her with his shoulder. "Come sit with me and Ana."

Kase had a way of ordering his twin sister around with a smile. He could make a demand sound like a gentlemanly request, just like their dad, Sheriff Ric Kasun. Willa loved her brothers and her alpha father, but there were days her heart ached for her mother.

"I think I'll pass." Willa straightened the hem of her top so that it met the waistline of her skirt. She hated the skimpy cheerleader getup, but until this year, she'd loved cheering for Kase at football games. If only he hadn't recently hooked up with one of the co-captains, Ana Novak.

As if Willa's junior year hadn't started off badly enough, she had been yanked into the seat next to Ana in history. She didn't have enough empty brain space to listen to another cheer idea or dreamy remark about her brother.

"I think I'm going to try something new this year." To make her choice clear, Willa tucked a piece of black hair behind her ear, making her edgy bob look even more fierce, and shot a smile at her brother. She didn't wait for him to respond, and turned toward the most supernaturally diverse table in the lunchroom.

As she approached, Willa recognized a few of the occupants from her earlier classes. Most of them had grown up in the same small town, and with that came rumors and stereotypes. A witch, Scarlet, noticed Willa first. Scarlet's long red hair swung over her shoulder as she looked back and forth from Willa to the empty seat next to her.

"Is that seat taken?" Willa asked.

Scarlet's lips parted, and one eyebrow pulled up in wonder. "Well, uh—"

A lean, white-haired guy slid between them. "No, it's not taken." He patted the seat and grinned. "Join us. I'm Tarron, and you're in my history class, right?"

Willa had seen the freckle-faced guy earlier, but his boyish grin contradicted his broad shoulders and square jaw. Tarron had sat at the back of the classroom, quiet with his pen to paper, not giving any attention to the reunions taking place after the three-month summer break.

Willa had thought the excitement overrated. She'd seen her pack throughout the summer and run into the other students at the Burger Bar and Coffee Haven, not to mention Paddlefest. The annual summer rafting event on Mathews River had come with extra tourists and drama this year. The pack dared Willa to swim against the river's current, and while the others used their wolf-strength, she couldn't dog-paddle five feet without revealing the fact that some of her powers were manifesting. She'd promised her dad she'd keep the development between them. That night, after her brother jumped into the water to pull her out, she felt so humiliated she moved out of her childhood home while her wolf pack enjoyed the bonfire.

"Hi," Willa greeted. She maneuvered around Tarron and sat between him and Scarlet, setting her bag in her lap. "And, yes, I think we do have history together, but you two," she pulled an apple out of her messenger bag and pointed it at a blonde girl with alabaster skin and the young dragon shifter who'd growled a few moments ago, "aren't in Ms. Bast's history class?"

Her apple bounced in the air back to the blonde, before she took a bite. The blonde nodded with the hint of a smile.

"You're new, too, aren't you?" Willa asked after swallowing, but then the blonde's mouth turned down as she realized her mistake. Willa sensed something supernatural about the new girl, and her cool stare and the scent of blood when she unscrewed her "water" bottle confirmed the stranger was a vampire. Willa set her apple down, wiped her hand on her skirt, then held it out. "I'm sorry. The sort I tend to hang out with don't pay much attention to manners. I'm Willa Kasun."

The blonde's stony palm slipped into Willa's warm one. "Hi, I'm Elliot. Well, most people call me Elle."

Just as the new girl shook Willa's hand, the table at the center of the lunchroom burst out into laughter. The Kasun pack's antics served them well on the football field and in the forest on a moonlit night, but trash talk and arm wrestling in the cafeteria had led to busted tables and busted lips in the past.

"See what I mean?" Willa joked. "It's probably my twin doing his impression of the biology teacher."

The growling guy leaned in and scanned the area. "So, you're the shifter girl from the Kasun pack who can't, you know—" He snarled and cupped his hands above his ears, mimicking a wolf. Willa thought they must all be supes if he felt confident enough to bring up her sort of being a werewolf, but she played it safe anyway.

"Can't what?" Willa's eyes narrowed, and her blood began to boil. She took the pendant hanging from her necklace between her thumb and finger, and slid it back and forth. A calming, methodical motion she'd perfected since she'd received the gift.

"Bale didn't mean anything by it." Tarron leaned in and nudged Willa's shoulder with his. "Did ya, big guy?"

Bale shook his head, and she caught a half-smile before a curtain of shoulder-length dark hair fell forward. "Nah."

"What Bale meant to ask is, how did you get out of wearing one of those gigantic bows the other cheerleaders are wearing?" Tarron nodded in the direction of Ana and her friend Maria, both giggling at Kase. "Are you sure they're not the twins?"

Everyone chuckled, including Willa. Then she caught her brother looking their way. She quickly moved her attention back to Tarron and bumped him back with her elbow.

"The co-captains were pretty ticked when I chopped off my

hair right before cheer camp, but those bows are a hazard when I'm flying or tumbling."

"I like it." Tarron smiled as his gaze slid from the top of her head to her cheer uniform.

Bale looked up. "Flying?"

His question broke her own examination of Tarron. "When they throw me up in the air. Wolves tend to like it on solid ground, but I'm not like the others." Willa picked up her apple and took another bite. "And, for the record, I may not have shifted yet, but that doesn't mean I'm any less a Kasun."

The defense she'd built over the last few years sounded rehearsed, and for good reason. Willa repeated the same words to herself whenever a pack member doubted her. She'd moved out of the pack's community in the forest more than a month ago. It hurt too much to be surrounded by a world she couldn't be a part of. Her dad knew the bullying had become intolerable, and he spent most nights with her. It was the best way to keep the rest of the pack from noticing her developing strength and speed, while he secretly investigated if there was another reason for her not shifting yet. Being away from the skeptics and having most of her family's support kept her anxiety at bay.

"So, Elle, where are you from?" Willa asked, trying to divert the eyes from her.

Bale's eyes widened. "Oh, don't start the list again."

Elle giggled.

"Hey." Scarlet pointed a finger at Bale. "Let the girl speak. I don't want to have to use this."

"You can't, and you wouldn't." Bale ran his hand through his hair, revealing a handsome face with high cheekbones and full lips. "Anyway, you'll just get all sad that you haven't been to any of the places she has."

Elle looked from Bale to Scarlet to Willa. "How about I keep it simple? I'm from a little bit of everywhere. My family came to Havenwood Falls so I could finish high school with my own kind. But I've never had vamp friends before, so I don't know why they think I'd want them now."

"Well, I'm glad you came to sit with us," Tarron said to Elle. "None of us are misfits, except maybe Willa here, but we like it here with each other more than our own." He shrugged and pressed his lips together into a tight smile.

Willa filled her mouth with another chunk of apple, trying to keep her retort to herself. She didn't know if Tarron was flirting or trying to allude to something else. Willa remembered her oldest brother, Conall, telling her that other supernaturals had a way of knowing things they had no business knowing. Maybe Tarron was referring to her moving out of the family's cabin.

But she couldn't be the only one with family issues. She regularly heard humans complaining about curfews and siblings as she maneuvered the halls between classes.

"What's so bad about the elves?" Willa asked Tarron and noticed his jaw tense. "Or the witches?" She turned to Scarlet to avoid Tarron, then looked at Bale. "Or the dragons?"

"What's so bad about the Kasun werewolves?" Tarron pushed back, but didn't sound angry. His mockery wasn't lost on her, though.

"Point taken," she conceded. Something about being different kept her and the others from revealing *how* different they were. No one at the table made eye contact, and Willa realized her social skills needed help. "Can I try this whole first-impression thing again?"

Tarron inched closer to Willa on the bench and nodded for her to proceed, while everyone else at the table gave her silent permission. A cacophony of teenage hormones and competing voices served as background noise until she came up with a question to redirect their conversation.

"So, what did you guys do for fun this summer?" she asked, forcing a smile.

"Hmmm..." Bale rubbed the stubble along his chin. "I

hiked up to the falls a few times, slept 76% of each day away, met a girl, and binged on Netflix. Is that basic enough?"

"You met a girl?" Tarron's eyebrows were lost in the fringe of white hair falling across his forehead.

Bale looked across the table at Scarlet, where his eyes lingered a moment too long. Tarron followed his gaze, and Scarlet fiddled with the hem of her skirt.

Willa leaned forward, blocking Tarron's line of vision, and propped her chin on her fists. "What about you, Elle? Did you move here from somewhere exciting, like New York City? I bet summers in the Big Apple are amazing."

As Willa took another bite of her apple, Elle twisted a few strands of her long blond hair between her fingers. "We actually moved here from Alaska. It was as cold and dark as it sounds, not that the cold really bothered me. Moving here and getting a tattoo that allows me to be out in daylight was the highlight of the last decade for me."

Tarron cleared his throat, and all eyes turned to him.

"Don't do it," Bale warned Willa, folding his arms over his chest. "Don't ask him about his summer. Tarron is baiting us."

"Why would he want to—" Willa was cut off when a hand slapped the table. The sound startled her.

Kase.

His bicep flexed as he leaned over the table.

"Hey, guys," Kase gritted, his face straining to maintain a smile. "Will, I need to talk to you."

"Will-*a*," she growled back.

"Willa, a word?"

Willa reached past Tarron and placed her hand over Will's. "Sure thing. How about after practice?" She squeezed, released it, and looked to Tarron. "My new friend here was about to tell us what he's been up to this summer."

Will's frown deepened in frustration.

"Hey, man," Tarron said to Kase. "You're more than welcome to join us."

Willa marveled at the two guys' familiarity with each other. Everyone in Havenwood Falls knew about each other, but it didn't mean they were friends. She wondered if her brother and Tarron had a class together. No. Tarron played football last year.

"No, but maybe I'll run into you on the field," Kase snarled at Tarron.

The elf leaned back in his seat and kicked his feet up. "Not this year. I'll be leading the archery team to State, instead of carrying the football team."

Kase flinched. "Come on, Willa, I never see you anymore. Eat lunch with me." His eyes inspected the table's occupants. "And I don't have the patience or time for whatever charity work you're doing here." It was a line straight from Ana's arsenal, her influence oozing out of him.

"Excuse me?" Scarlet seethed behind Willa, looking between the twins.

Willa stood, not amounting to much compared to her brother's six feet of muscle. "Shut your muzzle, Kase. I'm not sitting with or talking to you, because I'm tired of the crap your friends say behind my back. Every one of them thinks I'm a dud-wolf. For the past two years, I've only sat with the pack at lunch and cheered at football games for you. I'm doing this," she waved at the group, "for me."

Kase opened and closed his mouth without a sound.

"I'll talk to you after practice." Willa sat back down.

Kase blinked. "Fine." He walked back to Ana and let her coddle him with whispers and kisses, testing the strict no-public-display-of-affection policy.

"Well, he's a peach." Scarlet rolled her eyes. "How are you two related?"

Willa shifted in her chair. "He's not always that bad, just protective."

"Don't you have two older brothers, too?" Bale asked. "Deputies or something? That's gotta be rough."

"Yeah, one's a deputy and the other is still a cadet. They used to be more like Kase, constantly checking on me or giving me the third degree, but now they're too busy working," Willa explained.

"There's no way you can really be related to Kase." Tarron shook his head. "I still think those cheerleading bow-heads are the twins," he added with a grin.

And he winked at Willa.

CHAPTER 2

$\mathcal{W}$illa, surrounded by blue and silver pom-poms, spotted Tarron across the football field as she took her place at the top of the Wolf Wall Pyramid. She figured Ana chose the cheer stunt because of the name—one more way for her to slight any other supernatural in her midst. Tarron's white hair stood out in the sea of green grass past the blue jerseys as he stretched a bow and arrow in his hands. His muscles pulled taut as he aimed at a bale of hay painted with red circles. Tarron paused, glanced over his shoulder at the stacked cheerleaders, and released. The arrow pierced the small red circle at the center of the target. A human, Ginny, gasped as her eyes widened at the feat. When Tarron turned and saw her, he shrugged and acted just as surprised.

The crack of plastic football helmets smashing together startled Willa, and her twitch had a domino effect.

The pyramid shook. The girl holding Willa wobbled and pulled her leg. With the bend of her knee, the center of the formation crumbled. The co-captain, perched on the third level of their pyramid, tumbled down as well, and her backside thumped the turf. The wall had become a pile of bloomers and bows. Willa untangled herself from the pile of limbs and tried to escape blame by searching for her water bottle.

"Which of you inbreeds took your eyes off the mark?" Ana seethed as she stood. She pressed her hands down her skirt, not that it covered much. "We have a pep rally this Friday, and a game to follow. I will not be humiliated by one of you." Her pointer finger bounced up and down in front of her.

"It was my fault." Willa stepped forward. There weren't allegiances among the girls, and any of them would have outed her. They all pivoted to look back and forth between Ana and Willa.

Ana looked to her big-bowed best friend, Maria, then back at Willa. "Well, don't let it happen again."

The girls from the Kasun wolf pack had known each other all their lives, and everyone was practically family, but Ana had been trying to needle her way into Willa's immediate family for years.

"Of course. I'm sorry," Willa offered and twisted her lips. Apologizing was torture. "I think I need a break."

"I think she needs to head to the weight room," Maria said under her breath. The two girls giggled, and a few of the other girls joined in. Willa forced herself to wear a blank face. Standing so far away, she shouldn't have heard the snide remark. She picked up her messenger bag and cheer duffel, and waited for Ana to dismiss her. With a wave, Willa bailed.

They didn't know Willa could hear from so far away, or see Tarron so clearly across the field.

The pack was aware Willa hadn't shifted yet, and the town had quickly caught on when the kids her age started training, while Willa worked at her family's outdoor supply store. At the age of twelve, her friends in the pack, including Kase, all shifted for the first time and all received a special marking. The enchanted tattoos kept them from being hunted while in the forest, but they were also tied to wards at the high school enforcing a no-magic policy.

Because Willa hadn't shifted, she never went through the marking ceremony. So the wolf traits she'd developed, like heightened hearing, agility, and sense of smell, weren't being blocked on the field. She did wish her sense of smell was less heightened during football practice.

Even though her abilities were a secret between her and her father, the hint of power gave her hope the first few months. But by the end of her sophomore year, Willa had resigned herself to never shifting.

"Willa!" Her brother's voice called from a huddle of players as she walked down one of the racing lanes around the track.

She waved, only able to differentiate Kase by his number, and hoped he would leave her alone. As the starting quarterback, she had a feeling he wouldn't be able to get out of practice.

He'd pestered her every day via text to move back to the family cabin, but she'd been content in the apartment above Backwoods Sport & Ski. The family's store had belonged to them for a century, and while some of the pack members were employees at the town square shop, she still had privacy on the second floor.

Before she moved in, Willa's dad had used the space to hunker down when he was working on a case all night. Her dad still spent four nights out of seven on the couch in the living room, but this way Willa didn't have to wake up every morning and endure the inquisitive stares on her way to school. No one else seemed to care she'd moved, except Kase.

"Hey there, wait up." Tarron's voice called from behind her. "Why are you leaving practice early?"

"I guess my heart isn't in it today," Willa said with a hint of sarcasm.

One corner of Tarron's mouth pulled up. "Today?"

Willa burst out laughing. "I only cheer because of my brother. Otherwise, I would not be able to put up with the bow-twins."

It was Tarron's turn to laugh. "Ana Novak has been a

conniving bully since kindergarten. She talked me into giving her my vanilla pudding at least three times that year."

"What did she trade you?" Willa asked.

"That's the thing. It was always something disgusting, like carrot sticks."

Willa frowned. "That's horrible, but I can outdo you. So if I don't shift before my birthday in October, Ana will assume the position of alpha for our pack."

"No pressure." Tarron patted Willa's shoulder with a tight grin. "But, can a girl really be alpha? I thought your dad was in charge."

The comment earned Tarron a swift punch to the arm.

"Ow!" He rubbed his bicep and pouted. "That came out wrong. I like a woman who can take charge."

"Did that come out wrong?"

"Nope." Tarron winked at her again.

"My dad is standing in until I shift. But if I miss the cut off, the responsibility will be passed to Ana, since her dad is beta. My pack always had a female alpha—that is, before my mom died."

"Wait. Beta? Does that mean you're related?" Tarron's face soured. "She's dating your brother, right?"

"Beta means he's second in command." Willa tilts her head. "Our families are old, like ancient, so there's a good chance we're related. I think the Novak bloodline is related to Kasun blood from when our pack lived in Croatia. It's been several generations since our bloodline split, but it's the purest."

"Oh." Tarron shook his head. "It still sounds really bad. Kentucky bad."

The two chuckled as they approached the school's parking lot. A few students hung out in the lot, but fewer eyes watched them than the athletic fields behind the school. Tarron pulled his bow over his shoulder, against his quiver, and then started removing his arm guard. Willa's head tilted, inspecting the metal weapon and shooting gloves.

"What?" Tarron asked.

Willa shrugged. "I just thought your bow would be wooden."

Tarron placed his hands on his slim hips. "You're thinking about Lord of the Rings, aren't you?" He pulled his hand through his messy blond hair. It was long on top and shaved short around the sides. Willa thought she noticed a slight point at the top of Tarron's ears. "Sorry to disappoint, but I'm not glamouring waist-length hair or leather armor under here." Tarron motioned at his chest, covered by a graphic T-shirt sporting a taco with the words "Let's taco bout it."

"No need to be sorry, and if it makes you feel any better, I've never seen the movie. I've only read the books." Willa folded her arms across her chest.

"Impressive."

"Well, I've had a lot more time to myself lately. Living in town has its benefits, including more reading time and less fighting over Netflix." Willa fiddled with the strap of her messenger bag, wanting to ask Tarron if she could hold his bow. The request sounded crazy, and a little dirty in her head, so she filed it away for another time.

"Where do you live in town?" Tarron asked.

Willa turned down the sidewalk that led to the town square. "Off Eighth." She pivoted to walk backwards and smiled. "I'll see you tomorrow."

Stepping down onto the next slab of concrete, Willa didn't take into account the roots of an old oak having shifted the path or a student speeding out of the parking lot. She tripped into the street, the car screeching to a halt, but unable to stop fast enough. Tarron darted to her side. His reaction appeared in slow motion to Willa. She saw panic widen his eyes and fear pull the corners of his mouth into a frown. As he reached for her hand, she glanced at the driver of the car. Zara Shannon, a junior, jerked the steering wheel of her car to the left. Her friend, Viv, sat in the passenger seat and lifted her arms over her face. The front end of the blue vehicle still threatened to bash into Willa, and instinct kicked in. Willa flexed every muscle in her body, bending at the waist and changing the direction of her fall. She found her balance on the curb unnaturally.

Zara's car screeched to a stop and her head peeked out of the driver side window. Tarron shoved two fists into the air and bumped their sides together twice, successfully flipping off the girl like one of the characters from *Friends*.

Zara's mouth gaped open at Tarron as she started to get out. "Are you okay?" Zara asked Willa in an exaggerated British accent.

"I'm fine." She waved the human back into the car. "I promise." She placed her hand over her heart and felt it racing.

"You sure?" Zara asked as Viv opened her door.

"I am, thank you." Willa straightened the straps of her bags over her shoulders. "I'm good."

Willa tried to act distracted, hoping the two girls hadn't noticed her using her wolf abilities. They looked at each other, and Zara patted the top of the car.

"Well, if you're good, then . . ." She buckled back into the sedan, Viv following suit.

"Yeah, I'm good." Willa nodded.

"Okay, see you tomorrow." Her accent drifted off as they drove away.

Tarron turned to Willa and his eyes widened. "How did you—"

Willa ran her fingers along the chain of her necklace. "I can explain."

"We're still on school grounds, and the wards—" Tarron pointed to the Havenwood Falls High signage less than twenty feet away. His eyes narrowed, and he shoved his hands into his pockets. "Go ahead, start explaining."

"I really gotta get home. How about I explain tomorrow? Or, we could forget about it?" Willa scrambled to get out of telling Tarron the truth. She figured she could trust him with town gossip, but keeping the secret about her abilities was a level of trust she hadn't even given her brothers. The most she knew about Tarron was that he liked to flirt and could hit a target without looking.

"How about you explain while I walk you home?" Tarron suggested.

"I don't want to inconvenience you." Willa started walking, annoyed at herself for being so careless. "Thanks, though."

Tarron followed. He met her pace and remained five steps behind her all the way to First Street. Along the way, he started whistling. The tune floated on the August breeze and lulled Willa's footsteps into a steady cadence.

Willa tried to ignore Tarron, watching the cars pass by and the townspeople of Havenwood Falls tidy their yards. One neighborhood on the outskirts of town—Havenwood Heights—had become primarily exclusive to the Old Families, but the streets surrounding the town square were more like a mixed bouquet of wildflowers—supes ingrained in the everyday, normal lives of the townspeople. Tourists who made their way to town couldn't tell that a witch lived down the street from the town drunk, and if she was being honest, Willa wouldn't be able to tell either if it weren't for her wolf instincts.

Willa passed a man mowing his lawn and waved. The burly, bald guy had spent a few nights in the town's holding tank for getting too loud after a few drinks earlier that summer. Willa had brought her dad dinner at the station, and the man had made a pass at her. She'd laughed it off, but her dad threatened to charge him with indecent behavior with a juvenile.

At the end of the block, a street sign reading "2nd Street" towered over Willa. She waited under the metal guidepost for a car to pass, and Tarron stepped up next to her. He happened to be on the opposite side of the metal pole, and Willa remembered elves and faeries having an aversion to iron. He stood almost a head taller than her, and when he looked down in her direction, he smiled. Dark freckles peppered the bridge of his nose and cheeks, each a stark contrast to his pale complexion and hair.

"Can I ask you a personal question?" Tarron asked.

Willa folded her arms over her chest and pursed her lips. "You can, but that doesn't mean I'll answer."

He nodded, "Fair." He rubbed his hand against the back of his neck, hesitating. "So, do you really want to shift and be the next alpha of the Kasun pack?"

Willa's head tilted to the side. No one had ever asked her what she wanted. "If I don't try and implement the training I've received, if I don't give myself over to the wolf, I'll be letting my whole family down."

"It just seems like a lot of pressure in addition to ACTs, driving tests, showing up to cheer for your brother every Friday night, not to mention any potential dating relationships on the horizon."

Willa let a snort escape her, and quickly covered her nose with a hand. "Ever since my twelfth birthday party, I've been living in the shadow of my brother. And, there's not one pack member who'd ask me out. I'm a dud-wolf. You wouldn't want to date me. I mean, you've only met *one* of my brothers."

"Actually, I think I met your oldest brother when I got pulled over for speeding this summer." Tarron grinned and stepped into the street. "He didn't seem that bad. With a little of my elf charm, I got off with a warning."

"No way!" Willa sped up to catch him. "You know one thing I do want?

Tarron paused in the middle of the street and turned to face her. "What?"

Willa had slightly softened toward the elf, but at her core, she felt the need to tread carefully. "To learn archery." She walked past him to finish crossing the street.

"Oh."

"What? Did you think I wanted a social life?" Willa laughed.

"Maybe I could help you with both."

Heat rose into her cheeks as she reached the sidewalk. Willa looked to the quaint blue house on the corner to keep Tarron from noticing. She admired how the white shutters and door made the place look anything but supernatural. Willa waved at a small woman watering plants on the porch, a witch with waist-length red hair. A white streak of hair grew from her temple, making it difficult to guess her age.

The witch waved back.

"You know Ms. Howe?" Tarron asked.

"Not really." Willa shrugged as they passed the white picket fence. "Her herb shop is a few doors down from Backwoods Sport & Ski, and I've watched her sweep the sidewalk in front of her store countless times. How is she related to Scarlet? I noticed her coming and going from the shop a few times."

"She's Scarlet's grandmother." Tarron nodded back at the house. "All the women in her family look alike. From a distance, I can't tell Scarlet's mom and grandmother apart. Her mom, Rose, doesn't have as many wrinkles, or as many talismans hanging from her neck."

Willa looked up at him, confused.

"You know, like the one you're wearing." Tarron nodded toward the necklace. "It's pretty. Did you get it from their shop?"

"I'm not sure who made it into a necklace, but the stone was my mother's." She looked down at the pendant. "Do you know what talismans do?"

Tarron shrugged. "It depends."

∽

Chapter 2.5

MONDAY 8:25 PM

Willa: Are you home yet?

. . .

9:04 PM **The BOY Version:** On my way
    Willa: Don't text and drive

9:49 PM **The BOY Version:** Ok, home
    Willa: Do you remember where dad had my necklace made?
    The BOY Version: Where is this coming from?
    Willa: Never mind, forget it
    The BOY Version: Wait . . .

10:13 PM **The BOY Version:** I just asked Tate
    Willa: Ugh. Why did you have to pull him in?
    The BOY Version: He was playing D&D online, he didn't even blink
    Willa: Fine
    Willa: What did he say?
    The BOY Version: It was mom's ring
    The BOY Version: Sheriff asked the Novaks to change the setting
    Willa: I hate it when Tate calls dad Sheriff
    Willa: Maybe I'll change Tate's name in my phone to Sheriff
    The BOY Version: Give him a break, it's his way of dealing
    The BOY Version: Kinda like you moving out
    The BOY Version: Curious . . . Am I still 'the boy version' in your phone?
    Willa: . . .
    The BOY Version: You need to get over yourself
    Willa: Same
    The BOY Version: And you need to watch out for that Tarron kid
    Willa: Same
    The BOY Version: SMH
    The BOY Version: Love you
    Willa: Same

CHAPTER 3

*W*illa held her topaz stone at the end of her necklace and pulled it from left to right while she waited for the bell to ring. Students scrambled into the classroom, hoping to avoid a tardy notice being emailed home on the second day of school. She made a point to sit at the center of the pattern of desks, in a neutral and new seat.

A brunette girl bounced in, then a tuft of white hair caught Willa's eye. Tarron, wearing a T-shirt with a kitten roaring on his chest, strutted to the empty chair next to her.

"Is that seat taken?" he asked.

"Nope." Willa looked down at her black T-shirt with white bold letters. It read, "The book was better."

Tarron sat with a grin.

"What?" Willa asked with a furrowed brow.

Tarron's grin spread into a wide smile. "Good morning."

The bell sounded, distracting her from the knowing look he gave her, and their new history teacher, Ms. Bast, stood. She began drawing shapes on the whiteboard behind her desk. Her black-and-white-checked capris and fuzzy yellow cardigan would have aged anyone else fifty years, but Ms. Bast pulled it off with the help of a messy bun, black-rimmed glasses, and red ballet flats. Her warm brown skin glowed, even in the unflattering florescent light. The new teacher had to be the youngest person on staff at Havenwood Falls High.

Tarron leaned to the side and whispered, "Wanna come by the archery fields after cheer practice today?"

Before she could answer, a low, familiar growl vibrated in the air around her. Kase had run into the classroom and frozen at the sight of his sister and the elf sitting together. He quickly took the seat in front of Willa.

"Sorry, Ms. Bast," he apologized as he pulled a notebook and pen from his backpack.

"Don't make it a habit, Mr. Kasun." The teacher continued scribbling on the board. She grinned, her pearl-like teeth a stark contrast to her mahogany lipstick and bronze cheeks.

Kase swiveled in his chair and placed his elbow on Willa's desk. "Of course, Ms. Bast. Besides, I wouldn't want to lose my favorite seat in the room again."

His eyes flashed gold at Tarron, and he curled his lip.

"Give it a rest, Kase." Willa folded her arms across her chest and avoided making eye contact by focusing on the board.

Ms. Bast had sketched five different masks and started on a sixth. A few of the patterns appeared African, and one looked like it belonged on an Egyptian mummy. The next drawing only covered the eyes, like it would be worn to a masquerade, then she drew a few helmets. A total of ten masks covered the board when she finished and faced the students.

The class had started speculating about the drawings, and the layered whispers had grown into a rumble.

Ms. Bast cleared her throat. "Through the centuries, mankind has gone to great lengths to hide themselves. Some would argue helmets are for protection. Others might say masks allow for someone to be who they really are without being judged." She paused as her gaze drifted over the class. "Today I will be assigning partners for a project due at the end of the month. The presentation and paper you turn in will be worth half of your grade this six weeks. Every pair of students will be researching one of the masks on the board."

Ms. Bast picked up a stack of worksheets and gave a few to the first person sitting at the front of each row. The papers slowly made their way back to Willa, and she perused the instructions as she passed the stack behind her.

"Remember, deception is ultimately a disguise, and some facades give the illusion of sameness, so I'll be mixing things up to keep everyone honest. Let's start with Elle."

Everyone looked up at the new girl sitting on the front row.

"You'll be working with one of Havenwood Falls' natives, Kase."

Ana, who sat with the rest of the pack, huffed and jutted her chin in the air, and Will's buddy Joseph burst into laughter. Kase cut his eyes at the linebacker, silencing him.

Ms. Bast continued to pair students, surprising the class a few times by mixing supernatural races. Willa especially enjoyed Ana's name being called with Aurelia Petran. It wasn't until she heard Tarron's name that she realized how much she wanted to be paired with him.

She liked him.

The feeling wasn't like anything she'd heard a pack member describe with their mates, but Willa genuinely wanted to get to know Tarron better. She smiled to herself.

"Maria Horvat, you and Tarron will be working together on this helmet." Ms. Bast pointed to an open-sided, flat hat.

Willa's shoulders slumped, and her chest tightened with envy.

"As for this mask, I'd like Bale Grayson and Scarlet Howe to partner up."

Willa looked over to Bale, who was peering at Scarlet. She didn't bother to look over her shoulder. In the corner of her eye, Willa saw Maria's hand waving in the air.

"Yes, Ms. Horvat. Do you have a question?"

"No. But I do have a doctor's note specifying that I cannot

be exposed to anxiety-inducing situations, so I would like to be paired with someone else."

"You would?"

Maria nodded.

Willa looked over at Tarron, and he'd pinched the bridge of his nose between two fingers. She set a hand on his shoulder and asked, "Are you okay?"

"Would you be okay if you had Maria as your partner for a project worth half your grade?"

"I guess not." She patted him reassuringly. "I'm sorry."

Ms. Bast looked at the list of students in front of her, then glanced over the sheet of paper toward Maria. One more glimpse at the list, then an inspection of Tarron.

"Ms. Willa Kasun, would you be so kind as to partner with Tarron?" The teacher readied her pen over the paper. "I had planned for you to work with Joseph, but I think he's better suited to Maria's predisposition."

"That is fine with me," Willa answered, working hard to keep her smile to herself. She itched to look over her shoulder at Maria, but looked over at Tarron instead. A giddy expression lit up his face, and the thought of Tarron wanting to be her partner, too, made the classroom suddenly warm. And then she remembered her hand on his arm.

Struggling with what would be more awkward, she decided to pull her hand back, and then Tarron placed his hand over hers. The contact left her skin tingling.

"You'll have the rest of class to discuss your project, but after today I expect the work to be done on your own time. Tomorrow, come to class having read Unit 1, and be ready to tackle the beginning of time through 600 B.C.E."

The class erupted into a roar of voices trying to talk over each other. Students swapped seats and settled in with their partners. As everyone began working, the chaos quieted into a harmony. A few partners sat in silence, including Ana and her moroi partner. The mean girl of the wolves and the mean girl of the vamps had never been so quiet. Other pairs argued, like Maria and Joseph.

Willa inspected the room, focusing her attention on anything but Tarron. Her fingers found her pendant as she finally pulled enough courage together to face him. His eyes were already on her, not staring but observing. He rubbed his chin as if he were trying to figure her out.

"So, where do you want to meet?" Willa asked. "Your house?"

Tarron's eyes widened. "I'm not sure that's such a good idea. How about your place?"

"I don't think you'd get off with a warning if my dad or one of my brothers caught you up in my apartment."

Tarron picked up his pencil and twirled it between his fingers. "Well, if you still want archery lessons after practice, I guess we could discuss the project then. Maybe plan a trip to Broastful Brew later this week?"

Willa wanted to say yes, but she noticed her brother watching them. Will's lip curled, and she didn't know if her brother was mad or disgusted at having a vampire for a partner. The two supernatural species had been natural enemies in the world, but within the city limits, peace among the races reigned.

"So, what's so special about that necklace?" Tarron interrupted her thoughts.

"This was my mother's stone. My dad had it made into a pendant for me."

"It looks old," he said. "Can I take a closer look?"

Tarron lifted a hand to take the stone from her, and their fingers brushed against each other. He leaned in closer, inspecting the golden rock. The color reminded Willa of the shade a shifter's eyes flashed when close to releasing their wolf.

"I can take it off if you want to get a better look," Willa offered.

Tarron smirked. "I like this view."

But, he wasn't looking at the stone anymore. He'd met her eyes.

She snickered.

"Too cheesy?" he asked.

"Just a little." She held up her finger an inch above her thumb. "Do you ever give up? Or are you eager for disappointment? You have to realize that all your flirting won't get you anywhere."

"As long as it gets you to the archery field after school, I'll feel like I've accomplished something."

"Low expect—" Willa started.

"No." Tarron took her hand, and people in the room noticed. A hush fell over the classroom, and Tarron whispered, "Baby steps."

The self-deprecating tactics Willa typically used to avoid a guy's advances weren't working with this elf. He pushed past her walls and landed too close to her heart for comfort.

His warm hand slid off hers, and he went back to spinning his pencil like a baton. The silence between them had been compounded by the curious stillness of their classmates. Seconds dragged into minutes, and Willa resorted to doodling arrows along the side of her notebook.

The bell rang, announcing the end of class, and Tarron stood to leave.

Willa reached up for his hand and met his gaze. "I'll be there."

CHAPTER 4

*S*itting in the bleachers, waiting for the squad to disband, the football field to clear, and the white-haired boy with the bow and arrow to wave her over, Willa thought about the best part of her day. It had been lunch, again. She'd sat with her newly acquired Scooby gang. Of course, they all argued about who would be cast in which roles, and since Willa hadn't shifted yet, Bale claimed to be the best Scooby. When Tarron declared he would make the perfect Shaggy and Willa exuded Velma, the conversation stuttered. Elle was the first to break out into laughter, and the others joined in quickly.

An elf and a werewolf being anything more than acquaintances would be social suicide. Tarron had flirted with Willa, unashamedly, but there couldn't be anything more than friendship between them. Hence, Willa's reasoning for casting herself as Scooby. They could end up the best of friends, but someday Willa would shift. And with the pack came impenetrable devotion, fierce protection, and a mate.

Willa spaced out trying to remember a Kasun pack member who mated with someone outside their supernatural race. Conall, her oldest brother, was the only one who'd mated, but Tate once had a fling with a witch. It had been the summer before Kase and Willa turned twelve. They wouldn't have started high school for another year, but she understood a stigma came with stepping outside your coven, pack, or gene pool.

Willa remembered asking Tate, "Why do you like that witch?"

Tate pinched his nose and shook his head. "It feels good to be liked for me, and not the Kasun name, or the expectation that comes with it. Everyone struggles to fit in, but if someone wants to be with you because you aren't like everyone else, hang on to them." He mussed her hair. "Someday, you'll understand."

Willa now grasped what her brother had told her all those years ago.

"Hey, you coming?" Tarron called from the lined track.

Willa shook her head to clear it.

"Oh." He turned and started walking away.

"Wait, no!" Willa stood and maneuvered down the bleachers awkwardly. "I was in a daze, and I didn't see you wave me over."

"Really?" Tarron smirked. "You must have been thinking about someone pretty dreamy."

Willa ignored the innuendo and began the trek to the archery field. "Are you ready to multitask?"

Tarron jumped in front of her and walked backwards. "I think you'll find it's crucial to focus when wielding a weapon. How about we head over to the Burger Bar after I show you a few things?"

Willa tilted her head, wondering if the invitation was meant to be a date.

Tarron pivoted to walk beside her. "We can do a little recon on the helmet we were assigned and decide how to split up the paper we have to write."

"Yeah, um, that's a good idea," Willa agreed, but only because she could explain it away as a study session if anyone asked.

Tarron's lesson in archery started with a demonstration. Willa watched as the muscles in his arms stretched and tightened. His feet, clad in worn-out black Converse, were planted shoulder-width apart with one in front of the other. He took a deep breath and his chest widened.

Something buzzed at Willa's core, and the corners of her lips lifted. Being attracted to Tarron didn't feel wrong or weird. It felt good.

Releasing his grip with an exhale, Tarron froze in place until the arrow struck its target. He turned to face Willa, and his smile reached his gray-blue eyes. The arrow jutted from the center of the solid red circle.

"Your turn."

Willa's mouth fell open. "Are you sure I'm ready?"

"Nope, but you definitely need to get a feel for the bow while we're out here."

Willa had expected him to tease her or flirt, but on the archery field, Tarron had grown more serious than she'd ever seen him. His brow flattened as he pulled an extra shooting glove from his bag and strapped it to her right hand.

"How did you know I was right-handed?" She asked.

He didn't stop to think about it, but answered, "I'm observant." And he winked.

The playful elf Willa had grown to like hadn't gone anywhere. Tarron focused, and as his fingers gently tugged the glove down to her wrist, his mouth tightened into a straight line. As he concentrated on tightening the band, a few strands of his hair fell in front of his eyes.

Lifting her left hand, Willa tucked the hair behind his ear. She paused when her fingertip grazed the top. His ear came to a point like the petal of a flower and was just as soft.

"Does it weird you out?" Tarron asked softly.

Willa's eyes met his. "Not at all." Her lungs felt empty and full at the same time. She hadn't ever been so close to a guy, except for her brothers.

With a tug on the leather strap, Tarron stepped back.

"I think you're ready." After handing her his bow, he moved

out of the way and rubbed the back of his neck. Avoiding eye contact, he said, "Let's take a few minutes and work on your posture. If you decide to get a bow of your own, it will probably be smaller and lighter."

Willa was pretty sure he hadn't meant the comment as a slight, but being the youngest of four and the only girl, she took his words as a challenge. She lifted Tarron's bow and squared her shoulders. It took a little of the strength she normally hid, but she pulled back on the string and pretended to aim at the target.

"Nice, but—" Tarron pressed his fingertips upward, along her elbow.

Surprised at his touch, Willa released the string and her elbow snapped back into Tarron's chest.

"Oh, crap! I'm so sorry!" She set the bow in the grass and quickly lifted her gloved hand to Tarron's chest. She rubbed circles where her elbow had hit him and kept her eyes down.

"It's okay," he assured her softly as he caught her wrist.

Willa's eyes watched as his hand slid to cover hers against his chest. She blinked, and as she looked up to meet his eyes, her feet shuffled closer to his.

A whistle from an onlooker sounded from behind Tarron. Willa pushed up on her tiptoes to glance over his shoulder and watched as Kase, Joseph, and a few of their teammates strutted toward them.

Willa patted Tarron's chest and asked, "Will you let me handle them?"

"Sure, but say the word, and we're out of here." Tarron moved around Willa and picked up his bow.

Willa made her way to the track to meet her brother and keep him as far away from Tarron as possible. "Hey, Kase, you headed home?"

"Yeah." Kase squinted past her to watch as Tarron packed away his glove and arrows. "What are you still doing up here?"

"Oh, just working out some details about the history project." Willa twisted her hands together and felt the leather glove still strapped on her right hand. Carefully sliding her hands behind her, she shoved them into her back pockets. The evasion didn't fool her brother.

"What you mean is, he used the excuse to get you here for a study session, and now he's giving you archery lessons and using his elvish sorcery to get close?" Kase shouted over his sister at Tarron, "Normally, I'd be impressed. But if you try anything with my sister, I'll make sure your life is miserable."

Willa's lips twisted, unsure of what to make of her brother's accusations. "Sorcery?"

"You know," Kase kept on, "his charm."

"Magic isn't allowed on school grounds," Willa defended.

"True," her brother agreed. "But we can't help it if a little seeps out every now and then. Isn't that right, Number 22?"

"22?" Willa asked.

"It's why your boy here quit the football team," Kase pressed.

Tarron had picked up his bag, along with hers, and met them on the track. "I don't know what you're up to, but give it a rest. Your sister and I have to work with each other on the project, and it's none of your business why I'm not playing this year. You're just angry because you'll actually have to throw this year for the team to win."

Kase made a threatening move toward Tarron, and he dropped the bags, ready to defend himself. At the same time, Ana and Maria came around the corner of the building, looking for their ride home.

"Come on, Kase!" Ana whined.

Kase looked from his girlfriend to his sister. "I'm not leaving without her."

He crossed his arms over his chest, looking more like a stubborn toddler than a concerned brother.

"Don't be a bully," Willa warned. Her chest started to grow tight, and a burning sensation warned her that her wolf was close, but still out of reach.

Ana jogged over to them, with Maria not too far behind. She

placed her hands on her hips impatiently and huffed. "This is ridiculous. If she wants to stick around with the imp, so be it. We have stuff to do."

She placed a hand on Will's shoulder and tugged. Kase tugged back and ignored Ana.

"I'm not leaving without you." He spoke directly to Willa.

Willa looked from Tarron to her brother, not wanting to give in, but not wanting to make things worse. She reached for her pendant to calm her nerves and moved to stand next to Tarron.

Ana assumed Willa was taking a side. "Thank God!" She rolled her eyes. "I don't have time for this sideshow."

Willa squeezed her pendant and turned to face her pack. "It's a good thing Tarron and I are the main attraction then."

"Those are some big words coming from a girl who can't shift." Ana stepped in front of Kase and curled her lip.

"Do you need me to dumb it down for you?" Willa asked, then looked to her brother, hoping he would take the hint and leave with his girlfriend.

"You—" Ana growled.

"I'm done listening to you," Willa exclaimed. Her chest burned with power as the words left her lips, and the magic cut Ana off.

Maria took hold of Ana and stopped her from taking the confrontation any further. "She still has two months to shift."

"Like that's gonna happen." Ana waved dismissively at Willa and Tarron. "If she was going to shift, she wouldn't be wasting her time making toys with one of Santa's helpers."

Ana's insult provoked a snarl from Willa. Her wolf clawed at her insides trying to get out, but nothing happened outside. Being alpha had always been her destiny, and now she might actually have the chance to choose her own path. The problem was that the innermost part of her felt caged.

Willa had never been so mad before. Ana was so close to taking her pack, her future, and her brother. In the past, she'd struggled with being mad at her mother for dying, and later she blamed the powers that be for taking her away. Willa even hated herself for a time. She'd reconciled with herself by moving away from the pack.

"I may not ever shift," she admitted through gritted teeth, "but at least I won't have to live my life playing fetch for the Court of the Sun and the Moon."

Ana turned her nose up at Willa and hooked her arm through Will's, ignoring the dig. "Let's get out of here."

Unable to tamp down her anger, Willa interrupted, "No." She let go of her necklace and squeezed her hands into fists at her side. "You leave."

The command was palpable. The blood of an alpha ran through her body, and her words carried an unexplainable weight. They all felt Willa's power.

Kase stepped aside, out of Ana's reach, and looked at his buddy, Joseph. "Can you take them home?"

Joseph nodded.

"Come on, baby." Ana pouted. "Don't make me ride in Joe's truck. It's more ostentatious than your sister's necklace." She giggled and cut her eyes at Maria when her friend didn't laugh with her.

They had all attended the twins' twelfth birthday party. Each of them had watched Willa open the velvet box her father handed her, and they listened to the story he told of it belonging to her mother.

"How are you even with her?" Willa asked her brother with tears in her eyes.

He turned to whisper to Ana, and Willa heard something about leaving and talking later. Before she could listen to any more, Tarron placed his hand on her lower back. The distraction was welcome, but when she turned to face him, she knew something was wrong. He bit at his bottom lip and looked down at their feet.

"Why don't you go with your brother? It sounds like you

guys need to talk." He peeked up at her from behind a mess of hair and let a corner of his mouth turn up. "I'll take a rain check if you still want to go to the Burger Bar sometime."

"Give me your phone?" she asked.

He handed it over with his screen unlocked. Willa quickly texted herself. "Now you have my number, and I have yours."

By the time Willa finished and turned to face her pack, most of them had vanished behind the school building. Kase remained, waiting for her. He looked defeated, almost sorry.

Tarron started to leave, to give the siblings some time. As he walked by, a low growl rumbled in Kase's chest.

"Kase," Willa warned, mustering the last of her energy. "Stop." And he did.

Her brother moved to her side and took her bag from her. He'd already strapped his backpack and duffel across his shoulder, so what was another messenger bag?

Walking to the parking lot, Willa thought things had never gotten this complicated between them. The reason she'd left their community in the forest wasn't his fault, not entirely. She just hated how, in the last few years, he'd taken the pack's side.

Ana's side.

∾

Chapter 4.5

Tuesday 4:52 PM

Willa: Want to redeem your raincheck this Friday night?

5:04 PM Tarron: Shouldn't we get together b4 then about the project?

Willa: Don't think you're getting out of teaching me archery lessons that easy . . . We can talk then

Tarron: Ok, see you tmw

WEDNESDAY 11:28 AM

Tarron: Is it possible for your bros hate for me to grow daily?

Willa: Yes. It's because you sat next to me in history again.

Willa: Save me a seat at lunch.

6:37 PM **TARRON:** You did a good job today

Willa: Thanks! I'm going to try to convince my dad I need a bow over dinner tonight

Tarron: Good luck . . . leave my name out of it

9:43 PM **TARRON:** How did dinner go?

Willa: He's thinking about it. Ugh.

Willa: I just showered Wikipedia and found out our helmet is called a Kettle Hat!

Willa: Stupid autocorrect! I spelled scoured wrong!

Tarron: LOL!

THURSDAY 2:24 PM

Willa: I have to cancel today! I'm sorry!

Tarron: You ok?

6:14 PM **WILLA:** Yeah, just had some errands to run after school

Willa: I have a surprise tmrw!

Tarron: Please tell me you're wearing a big bow, no don't, I want it to be a surprise

Willa: LOL! G'night

Willa: I almost forgot . . . Do you want to leave the game tmrw night together and head to Burger Bar?

Tarron: . . .

Willa: We can meet if you're not planning to come to the football game

Tarron: I'll be there . . . Wouldn't miss it

CHAPTER 5

*T*he crowd of blue and silver cheered their way out of the Havenwood Falls High School stadium. The first victory of the season would spill over to the Burger Bar, and Willa looked forward to downing a chocolate milkshake and greasy cheeseburger.

Even though it was the first day of September, the summer heat continued to press on. As the sun set, the cool night air calmed the restless fans. Willa searched the bleachers for Tarron and didn't see him until the last quarter. She looked forward to hanging out somewhere other than school and wondered if they'd have enough in common to carry a conversation through dinner.

"See you at the drive-in?" one of the other cheerleaders asked Willa.

"I'll be there," Willa answered as she bent down to stuff her pom-poms into her duffel. Rummaging around in the depths of her bag, she noticed a hint of body odor emanating from her armpits. "Hey, do you have some deodorant I can borrow?"

"I actually didn't think to bring any with me," Tarron's voice answered. He squatted down beside her and sniffed. "I think you smell okay, but you're the one with superscent." He smiled.

Tarron wore dark jeans, his Converse, and a gray-blue T-shirt that brought out the color of his eyes. Willa couldn't make out what his shirt said, because his hoodie was half zipped. She was relieved he hadn't made things more awkward by showing up in something more formal. The last four days had been uneventful, and the drama-free days had given Willa time to think.

"Are you ready?" Tarron asked.

"Yep." She zipped up her bag and lifted it, but he took it from her before she could place it on her shoulder.

"I've got this."

The path to the parking lot still buzzed with Havenwood Falls Dragons, so Willa took Tarron's hand and pulled him up to the bleachers. She'd been waiting all day to reveal her surprise, but the timing hadn't been right in history or at lunch.

"How about we hang out here until the lot clears out?"

Tarron followed her up to the top row. "Sounds like a plan."

Just as they sat, the stadium lights turned off with a loud clack. The two broke out into laughter, and as Willa's eyes adjusted to the sky above them, it blinked to life.

Scooting a little closer to Willa, Tarron asked, "So, what's the surprise you texted me about?"

She looked up at him with a wide smile and answered, "My dad said yes. He's letting me pick out a bow and arrows from the store."

"That's awesome." He bumped her with his shoulder. "Maybe I can swing by tomorrow and help you pick them out?"

"Oh, well, I have ACT prep in the morning, so it would have to be later."

Tarron grinned.

"What's so funny?" Willa asked defensively. "If I don't want to have to work at the store my whole life, I'll need a good score."

"I'm not making fun, Willa," he assured. "I'll be there too.

Actually, I think Bale and Scarlet are enduring the course with us."

"With four Saturdays of ACT prep and Friday night games, how are we going to get this history project ready?"

Tarron's grin spread wider. "I guess we'll have to spend a lot of time together."

Willa liked the prospect of studying with Tarron, and she didn't care if everyone else had something to say about it. People had been talking about her behind her back all her life. When she was little, she'd been called the poor little motherless girl, and during the past four years, she'd been referred to as the dud-werewolf.

"How about we spend some time together at the Burger Bar? I'm starving," Willa said.

She stood and grabbed Tarron's hand to pull him up. As she made her way down the bleachers, she attempted to release him, but he didn't let go.

They walked to the parking lot, now almost empty. Willa noticed a few of the players' cars waiting for their owners to shower and change. Her hand slipped out of Tarron's when she started walking down the sidewalk, toward the drive-in. Students frequented the place located across the street from the school throughout the week and especially on game nights. Positioned along the river, teenagers roamed along the water's edge, hooked up, and swam in the summer.

"Where are you going?" Tarron asked from a few feet behind her.

Willa paused. "Food." She pointed to the vintage neon sign in the distance. "Hungry." Her finger shifted to point at her stomach.

"Car." He pointed to a light blue vintage convertible parked at the back of the lot.

Willa stepped closer, looking for some kind of emblem on the hood. "Is it yours?"

"It is. It's a 1961 Corvette," he explained. Glancing at Willa, he noticed her eyes gloss over. "And that doesn't matter."

Willa shook her head and turned to face him. "It matters if you're a car guy." She glanced at the car, then back at him. "Go ahead, tell me all the stats. We can still be friends."

Tarron chuckled. "I'm really not that into cars. This one happened to belong to my dad, and he gave it to me for my sixteenth birthday."

Willa stopped in front of the car and stuck her hand out to shake his. "Hi, my name is Willa. Have I met you before? You look so familiar."

Taking her hand, he pulled her close instead of shaking it. "There is a lot you don't know about me, but with some time, I think we can remedy that."

Willa wanted to get to know him better, but the more time they spent together, the more she liked him. A year ago, she would have chalked Tarron up to a distraction. She'd been convinced that's all he was a week ago. His breath brushing across her ear called attention to the lack of space between them. Her smile flattened, and she closed her eyes to compose herself.

"Your cheeseburger awaits." Tarron stepped back and opened the car door for her.

Willa blinked and watched as he tossed her bag in the trunk. She slid into the passenger seat and grinned when Tarron made his way to the driver side and jumped over his door with supernatural grace. The engine roared with the turn of his key, and Willa leaned her head back to enjoy the breeze as they crossed the street.

The Burger Bar hummed with teenage hormones and souped-up trucks and cars. Tarron circled the lot twice before someone vacated a parking space. When he pulled in, Willa noticed the cars on either side of them were empty. Most occupants congregated inside or at the front of the drive-in, but some dispersed to a less rowdy location near the river.

"So, what can I order you?" Tarron's finger hovered near the call button.

"A cheeseburger, plain, and a large chocolate shake, please."

He placed her order and added a burger, strawberry shake, and tater tots for himself. Sitting in the car, waiting, Willa wracked her brain for something interesting to say. Subconsciously, she held the pendant of her necklace and pulled it from side to side along the chain.

Tarron unbuckled his seatbelt and shifted to face Willa. "Uh-oh, what's wrong?"

"What do you mean?"

"Well, you have a tendency to do that," he pointed to her neck, "whenever you get nerv—wait, do I make you nervous?"

A knowing grin spread across Tarron's face, and Willa couldn't decide if she wanted to kiss his full lips or run away more. She pushed both notions down and swallowed. Her throat had grown dry, but she needed to tell him the truth.

"Yes," she admitted. "It's just that I've never liked anyone before. All my life I thought I'd shift, become the alpha, and eventually find my mate. In less than two months, all of those plans will shatter if I don't shift. I'm starting to accept my fate, and the choices that come with it."

"And you don't want to make the wrong choice?" Tarron asked.

"No, I mean yes—" Willa covered her face with her hands.

A cute brunette wearing roller skates glided around to Tarron's side of the car with a tray full of food. "Hey, honey, that'll be $24.67."

Handing her two bills, he said, "Thanks, Maggie, keep the change."

She hooked the tray on the driver side window and winked at Tarron before skating away.

Willa pointed her thumb over her shoulder towards the trunk. "I have some money—"

"I've got this."

"But—"

Tarron handed her a large styrofoam cup. "You can pay next time, but only if you're the one doing the asking out."

"Hey! I asked you out this time." She took a long sip of her milkshake and cringed. Strawberry.

Tarron's face stretched into a similar frown after taking a drink from his cup. "Bleh, sorry." He handed over the chocolate milkshake to Willa. "I believe this is yours."

She handed him the strawberry shake and asked, "Do you want me to get you a new straw?"

"Nah, I think I'll be okay."

The two ate while debating which flavor of milkshake was best. The only flavor they could agree they both liked was vanilla. Willa stole a few tater tots, starting another discussion about which foods were appropriate to share. Both conceded to finger foods being acceptable, but anything eaten with a spoon verged on disturbing.

Tarron piled all of their trash onto the tray and set it under the intercom. He started the car and pulled out of the Burger Bar, set on a course to the town square. Willa didn't want the night to end. She enjoyed hanging out with someone who didn't know everything about her. It forced her to think through why she only liked whole strawberries, but not strawberry flavored food. And she had no clue what Tarron had against chocolate, but it made her question whether they could really be friends. The topic had made her laugh so hard her stomach hurt.

"Do you want to walk around the square with me?" Willa placed a hand over her belly. "I'm so full."

"Sure." Tarron got out and circled the car to meet her.

The night breeze had turned almost cold, but Willa had enough wolf in her to keep her warm. She walked toward the gazebo at the corner of the square, and as she came to the steps up onto the platform, Tarron's hand slipped into hers. She looked down, and thought no one in Havenwood Falls would be able to tell which of them was the werewolf or elf by just looking at their entwined fingers.

"Do you know any couples in town who are different supernatural races?" Willa asked.

"I do." He nodded and pulled her under the twinkle lights strung around the pavilion. "Why do you ask?"

There had to be couples in town made up of two races of supernaturals. Being raised in the forest by her pack, she hadn't been around any mixed-race couples. She'd seen a few in town now and then, and she understood some supernaturals didn't care about blending bloodlines. With tension constantly high between the werewolves and vampires, and witches, and hunters, and any other supe with an aversion to authority, Willa guessed wolf shifters were probably the last race another supe would want to date. Not to mention, she'd been groomed since birth to be alpha and hadn't ever considered the possibility.

Willa faced Tarron. She'd asked out of curiosity in general, but she also wanted to get his reaction. "There hasn't been a werewolf in the Kasun pack who's mated with another supernatural race that I've ever heard of, not to say they haven't dated another supe—"

"You're starting to ramble." He grinned and tucked a strand of hair behind her ear. "What do *you* want, Willa?"

"I think I want to change things, and not just for me," she answered, looking up to meet his gaze. "I want to put together a team of our friends to compete in the Founders Day Games."

Tarron blinked a few times, taken back by her answer. "Do they let teams with mixed supernatural races compete?"

"Sure, but not from the high school." She beamed. "Are you in?"

"Sure." He grinned at her enthusiasm. "Hey, have you ever thought about why there hasn't been a team from the high school before?"

Willa shook her head.

Tarron slid a little closer, his arm grazing hers. "Most kids want to feel normal, you know, fit in. And sticking with your own kind is an easy way to do that. It might be harder, but finding people who like you for more than your bloodline is real friendship."

"Friendship?" Willa tilted her head.

Tarron rubbed his hand along his jaw in thought. "Sure. Friends like Scarlet, and Bale, and Elle are not easy to come by." He grinned.

Willa understood what Tarron meant about wanting to belong. As the future alpha, she grew up wishing for the other pack members to accept her as one of their own. Instead, she felt the pressure of their expectations and the anxiety from not meeting them.

"Maybe, someday, I won't feel so bound by what everyone else expects, and I'll be free to go after what I want." Willa looked down at her feet.

"Someday?"

Willa's head slowly lifted, and her eyes met his. Her lips twisted in determination. "Ask me what else I want."

He tilted his head. "Okay, but I'm warning you, you can't have my car."

Willa tugged on his hand.

"What else do you want?"

"I want to kiss you."

Tarron's smile grew into a grin. He slid a hand around her lower back and pulled her closer. Willa pushed up on her toes and wrapped her arms around his neck. Tarron's lips gently pressed into hers, and she let her eyelids flutter shut.

Willa tasted cinnamon when Tarron kissed along her bottom lip. She didn't think she could be any closer to him, as her fingers traced his hairline along the back of his neck. Before he pulled away, he left a trail of kisses across her cheek, all the way to her ear. When he reached her neck, he whispered, "I wanted to kiss you, too."

His words stirred a growl in her chest, and Tarron chuckled.

"I'd better get home." Willa stated the obvious. She thought spending time with him would make her feel less awkward, but now they'd kissed. He'd been her first kiss.

Tarron held his hand out for her to take. "I'll walk you."

They made their way across the street, and Tarron grabbed Willa's duffel from his trunk. Once in front of Backwoods Sport & Ski, Willa dug around in her bag for her keys. She unlocked the door, and before stepping inside, gave Tarron a kiss on the cheek.

"Thank you for tonight. I'll see you in the morning."

"Good night." He stepped away.

From inside, Willa peeked her head out of the door. When Tarron jumped into the driver seat, she smiled. He had a similar grin stretched across his face.

"Hey! Tarron, I'm curious," she called before he had a chance to start the car. "Which couple do you know—"

"My parents."

The Corvette roared to life, and all Willa could bring herself to do was wave at Tarron as he backed out of his space.

Chapter 5.5

FRIDAY 11:52 PM

Willa: Thanks for tonight!

Tarron: I had fun . . . let's do it again soon

Willa: . . .

Tarron: Are you trying to figure out how to ask me about my parents?

Willa: I'm def curious, but don't want you to feel any pressure . . .

Tarron: My dad is an elf and my mom is a witch

Willa: Did they have to deal with any crap to be together?

Tarron: Not that I know of

Willa: It must be a wolf shifter thing

Tarron: The Kasun pack is known for being pretty tight

Willa: Yeah

Willa: Wanna save me a seat in the morning?

Tarron: Sure thing

SATURDAY 3:37 PM

Tarron: That was brutal

Willa: I knew the ACT would be hard, but the prep was so boring!

Tarron: You mean easy?

Willa: That too

Tarron: What are you doing?

Willa: Reading up on a certain helmet

Willa: Do you want to handle the paper or the presentation?

Tarron: Presentation, but I don't mind helping with the paper too

Tarron: I'll tell you about my idea when you try out your new bow Monday

Willa: Deal

MONDAY 7:44 PM

Willa: I totally thought I'd be better than I was! I'm going to need a lot of practice!

Tarron: What exactly are you referring to?

Willa: Archery, what did you think I meant?

Tarron: Archery, of course

Tarron: Don't worry, you're a quick study!

Willa: Will you help me with something this week?

Tarron: Will it require spending more time together and lots of practice?

Willa: I want to convince our Scooby gang to enter the Founders Day Games as a team

Tarron: . . .

Willa: If we play, I'll spring for Broastful Brews

Tarron: Lead with that

CHAPTER 6

ounders Day was always held on the autumn equinox, and this year that meant the Havenwood Falls High student body would get out of school on Friday. Willa had successfully convinced Tarron, Bale, Scarlet, and Elle to join her team for the games, but she'd have a big coffee order to fill. It wasn't until the day before at lunch that Willa dropped two bombs.

First, the team had to show up at the town square at eight in the morning. It was an hour earlier than what she'd initially thought.

Her announcement was met with groans from Bale, but the girls took it well. Every team needed to be informed of the rules, even though they were the same every year. The games never changed, and the teams from each supernatural race rarely changed. Everyone sought bragging rights for the year, and while it sounded silly for grown men and women to participate in a wheelbarrow race, it was oddly entertaining.

Willa also told the others that her twin, Kase, would be their sixth teammate.

The silence that fell over the table was followed with a snicker from Scarlet. "You're joking."

"No, we need one more player, and he promised to play nice," Willa tried to explain.

Bale folded his arms across his chest. "I hate to be the one to break it to you, but your brother hasn't played nice since we hit double digits."

"Come on, Bale. Let's try to give him a chance," Tarron said.

Willa woke up early Friday morning to the noise of Founders Day committee members setting up. She dressed in black joggers and a T-shirt declaring "coffee first." She walked past the storefronts of the square and stopped at the coffee shop. Scarlet found her balancing two cupholders full of caffeine.

"Are you ready for this?" Scarlet took one of the cardboard trays and set it on a nearby bench while she pulled her long red hair into a bun at the top of her head.

Willa watched as a group of vampires arrived and exited a black SUV. "Yeah, I think so."

Scarlet moved to block her view, with her latte in hand. "Can I ask you something personal?"

Willa nodded.

"Is forming this team about proving something to your pack in regard to Tarron or do you have another agenda?"

The question hit Willa in the chest and left her speechless for a few seconds. She'd told herself the team was about showing her classmates they could all work together. There didn't have to be outsiders or insiders. But an ache near her heart revealed that Scarlet was on to something.

"Can it be about Tarron and me *and* proving a point?" Willa asked.

Scarlet scooted to stand beside Willa, and they watched Tarron pull up in his convertible with Bale. "Just remember, proving you're right about him isn't about them. If you focus on proving them all wrong, you could lose him."

"Why are you and Bale hiding your feelings for each other?" Willa asked.

Scarlet's eyes grew wide. "How did you—"

"I just had a hunch."

Scarlet looked off at the cloudy sky. "It doesn't have anything to do with me hating on shifters, if that's what you're getting at."

"I didn't think so."

"It's just that women in my family have a knack for getting our hearts broken. Bale and I decided it would be better to move on when school started, and that way we could stay friends." Scarlet shoved her hands into her hoodie's pockets. "Do you mind not letting on about knowing anything happened between us?"

Willa mimed zipping her lips shut as the guys approached. Her mood lightened with Tarron around, but she couldn't help thinking about how self-absorbed she'd been, worrying only about her own problems lately. She would make it a priority to be a better friend to Scarlet going forward.

"Where do we check in?" Tarron asked as he approached them. He smiled and winked at Willa.

"I think we have to wait for everyone to get here before we register." Bale turned and searched the square. "There's Kase." He rolled his eyes and caught Willa watching him. Shrugging his shoulders, he moved to stand next to Scarlet and nudged her with his elbow.

"What was that for?" Scarlet asked with a smile.

Bale tucked a strand of hair behind his ear. "Just making sure you're awake."

The two didn't hide their chemistry well. Willa felt a couple vibe coming from them on the first day of school, and it grew stronger daily. Their eye contact always lasted a few seconds too long. Scarlet would pat or shove Bale's arm during conversations. And Bale always sat directly across from Scarlet. Willa wondered if they played footsie under the table without anyone noticing.

Kase met the group on the sidewalk, and Willa could tell he was mentally counting everyone who stood with her.

"We're still waiting on Elle," she said.

Just as she mentioned Elle's name, the blonde, lanky vampire strutted around the corner in jogging shorts, running shoes, and a Salt Life sweatshirt. When she caught sight of them, her face lit up, and then she noticed Kase. Elle's mouth immediately turned down, but her feet didn't falter.

"Finally," Kase murmured.

Willa slapped his chest with the back of her hand. "Be nice."

There was no reason to play into the werewolf versus vampire cliché. Elle had proven to be friendly every day at school, and she was the only one at their table who didn't flinch when Willa announced her brother would be a member.

The group walked across the street to the registration table together. A few curious eyes watched them. Willa specifically noticed her brother, Tate, standing in the gazebo at the corner of the square. His cadet uniform proved his purpose for being up so early, but Willa could see her older brother's disdain for being forced to patrol at the annual event in the frown stretched across his face. He typically looked twenty-five, even though he was born in 1917, but his misery made him appear as old as their oldest brother. Born in 1867, Conall resembled a handsome mid-thirties version of their father.

"Can I help you, dear?" asked Irene Beckett, a doughy, elderly woman with a nest of gray hair piled on top of her head.

"We'd like to sign up for the games." Kase stepped forward and flashed a grin in her direction.

While trying to separate two forms, Mrs. Beckett, the town's gossip, rambled, "We haven't had a group of young people from the high school play in ages." She passed the paper to Kase, and he handed it to Willa. "Plenty of *families*, all trying to prove their place in this town."

"Don't let her fool you. My sister's trying to prove something, too." He rolled his eyes.

Willa slapped him in the chest with the back of her hand, again.

After filling out each participants' name and age, Willa handed their form over, and the group waited for the games to begin. They watched as humans and supernaturals alike prepared for relay races and tug of war. Willa noticed some of the Court members wading through the growing crowd. Anyone familiar with the Court of the Sun and the Moon knew Founders Day was a way for the supernatural leadership to complete a census each year.

One of the leaders welcomed everyone and prattled through a list of events for the day. The games were always first, then lunch, and the reenactment typically started at dusk. But this year, they were re-opening the newly renovated library before the games.

"The three-legged race will begin in five minutes!" a deep voice shouted a while later, with the help of a bullhorn from the gazebo.

When Willa looked toward the voice, she saw Tate plug his ears with his fingers. A squat man, impeccably dressed in slacks, a light blue dress shirt, and suspenders, stood next to her brother and had propped the horn up in his direction. She giggled, and when he realized she saw him, he made his way toward her. The last thing she needed was two of her brothers mocking her new friends. Tate tended to be more understanding than Kase and Conall, and he had a stubborn streak similar to Willa's, but that didn't mean he'd take her side.

Willa, hoping to avoid introductions, jogged a few yards to meet Tate. "Hey!"

"Hey, yourself. How are you doing?" Tate wrapped his arms around her and picked her up. He was the tallest Kasun in the family, and Willa happened to be the shortest. Instead of stooping down for a hug, he always lifted her up.

"Things are good." She nodded in Tarron's direction when he set her on her feet.

Tate looked from Tarron to Kase to Willa.

"Er—As good as they can be." She grinned.

Tate laughed. "So, is he what inspired this public display?" He nodded to Tarron. "You've never wanted to compete before."

"Anyone is allowed to play." Willa propped a hand on her hip. "I just wanted to hang out with some friends . . ."

"And."

"And, I may be trying to prove a point. Let's be honest, after my birthday, I won't really belong anywhere."

"What are you talking about? You'll always belong with us."

"Saying it isn't the same as what I feel when I'm with the pack." Willa placed a hand on her temple and rubbed small circles. "When Ana's family takes over, I'm not sure I can—or want to—be a pack member. It will destroy Dad if they replace him as sheriff in addition to Ana being named alpha. And you and Conall, what will you do if the Novaks replace you?"

"It's kind of a scary thought for the town, isn't it? It won't bother me as much as the sheriff and Conall, but you shouldn't be worrying about us," Tate reasoned.

"I need to find a place for myself, but Havenwood Falls High has a way of keeping us all in our places."

"You don't have a place, and if you did, it wouldn't be here in this hellhole." Tate's chest rumbled. "You're better than all of this. Don't you remember what Elder Lav said over you at your twelfth birthday?"

Willa rolled her eyes.

"I know you don't think much of the pack, but our ways are a part of who you are. They will continue to be a part of who you become."

"But he's madder than any hatter, Tate. No one puts any stock in anything he says," Willa argued. "And how can you say all of that when you're wasting away working on the force?"

"I'm just waiting for Elder Lav's words to ring true."

"No pressure."

Tate smiled. "If it's written in the stars the way he foretold, everything will work out. The pack won't just endure, but we'll prosper."

"Live long and prosper." Tarron walked up behind Willa and

held his hand in the air with his middle and ring fingers separated.

Tate's head tilted to the side.

"Geek speak, sorry." Tarron held his hand out to Willa's brother. "Hi, I'm Tarron, and you must be a Kasun."

Tate shook his hand firmly. "Officer Kasun, when I'm wearing this." He pointed to his badge. "But when I'm off duty, Tate's fine."

Willa, impressed and perturbed at how quickly her brother could turn his Officer Stick-in-the-Mud persona off and on, shoved her brother.

Tarron squared his shoulders and spoke more formally. "So, Officer Kasun, what do the stars have to say about Willa?"

Tate looked to Willa for permission, but she just twisted her lips. Living in a town full of supernatural beings with super-hearing was annoying.

Clearing his throat, Tate began to recite the prophecy in a low dramatic tone, impersonating the ancient elder who roamed the Havenwood Falls forest. "In the stars is written the tale of a valiant warrior, a wolf who will lead her pack to harmony. The moon will call, but there will be no reply. In the silence, the alpha's mind will battle her heart, but courage will make her whole and shine, a beacon of hope . . . Er, something like that."

Tarron squinted his eyes and nodded slowly. "Impressive. I didn't know werewolves had prophets."

Willa crossed her arms over her chest. "There are stories about elders centuries ago who had special abilities, like seeing the future and mind reading, but Elder Lav's nickname is Loony Lav, if that gives you any idea of how seriously we took him. I think he predicted one of the pack members would also defy gravity someday."

"Don't let her fool you," Tate said. "There are a lot of us in the pack who are holding onto the hope Lav predicted."

"Three-legged race, starting in one minute!" A loud voice echoed across the town square.

"We'd better get going." Willa hooked her arm through Tarron's and started to pull him toward the games.

"Nice to meet you," Tarron offered, with a look over his shoulder back at Tate.

"You, too." Tate waved. "Good luck!" His eyebrows raised as he nodded at Willa. She knew he meant with her and not the Founders Day games.

Once they met the others, groups began to line up at the start. A bandana tied two team members together, and Willa anticipated they'd do well. There wasn't much strategy in running around a cone fifty feet away. Scarlet and Bale raced first and held their own with the more athletic competitors. Kase and Elle got off to a rocky start, but by the time they reached the cone, they'd fallen into sync. It was up to Willa and Tarron to make up the few yards they were behind, and with a last-ditch effort, the two threw themselves across the finish line in a dive.

"By the skin of their teeth, or more accurately by the tip of a finger, our team from Havenwood Falls High has taken their first win," the day's announcer reported. "Next will be the sack race."

In the excitement, Willa embraced Tarron. Scarlet gave Bale a quick hug, then pulled back. She looked around them to see who might have been watching. Kase turned to Elle and held his fist out for her to bump. She grinned and pushed her first two fingers under his fist.

"You get a snail fist bump, since we were the slowest of the crew." Elle's smile grew into a grin, and she laughed as Will's mouth turned down.

"Let's see who's the slowest in the sack race," he taunted.

The team of teens managed to scrape by with third place in the next race, but as they prepared for the tug of war, they began to fall apart. Willa couldn't put her finger on what was said, or who said it, but they went from encouraging each other to comparing their strengths and weaknesses. After each competition, they felt less like a team and more like six strangers.

By the end of the morning, they'd avoided last place, but landed in second to last. Tarron and Willa joked about the feat, but Kase stomped away, mumbling something about how embarrassed he was to be seen with them. Willa was proud of Tarron and Bale for keeping their mouths shut until her brother was out of hearing range.

"I'm not sure what he's complaining about. We ranked better than his precious football team has this season." Bale shoved his hands in his pockets. "I'm gonna get a burger. Wanna come with, Scarlet?"

His casual nod toward the cart on the street made Willa think he wasn't as worried as Scarlet about being seen together.

"See you guys later." She shrugged her shoulders, and the two walked away.

Elle, left standing with Tarron and Willa, examined the lawn around their feet. "Well, I think I'm going to head home." She pushed at the grass with the toe of her running shoes.

Willa didn't want Elle leaving on such an awkward note. "Are you sure? I think you should stay and hang out a little longer. We could get lunch and eat near the river. Doesn't that sound fun?"

Willa elbowed Tarron.

"Yeah!" Tarron sounded like a used-car salesman. "Stay and have lunch with us. You don't want to miss the reenactment later."

Elle shrugged. "I guess I could stay a little while longer."

The three walked up to the Burger Bar's grill and waited in line for their food. With grub in hand, they made their way down Eleventh Street to Mathews River. The area east of the ski resort had always been a haunt of the teenagers in town. There were picnic tables and park benches scattered along a path that ran parallel to the water.

"Nice job today!" Ana's voice called from the river's edge.

Willa rolled her eyes. "Thanks."

She hoped her minimal response would keep the interaction short. But she had no such luck.

"It's a good thing we all made it to see what a great leader you are." Ana gestured to the pack members with her. "I mean, we can't wait to be besties with vampires and—what are you, exactly?"

Ana had turned to speak directly to Tarron, but it was Elle who responded first. "You don't even know what you have here." She spread her arms wide. "Why would you waste living in this town and only be friends with shifters?"

Tarron and Willa looked at each other, then back at Elle. She was being sincere, and Ana laughed.

A growl grew in Willa's chest, and everyone but Tarron and Elle took a step back. Willa felt her supernatural power pressing against the inside of her skin, eager to be released. She curled her lip and snarled.

"What was that?" Kase asked as he walked up from the river.

Willa wanted to shift, right there, in front of everyone. But it would have been against so many of the Court's rules. Not to mention, she still felt like her magic wasn't enough. Not enough to shift. Not enough to be alpha. Not enough to keep up this charade.

"Nothing," Willa mumbled.

She walked away with Tarron and Elle on either side, wondering if she deserved to have them in her life. She glanced back at her brother and the others, knowing deep down she belonged with them. Kase wrinkled his nose as he watched them leave, and his eyes lingered on Elle. Willa had failed to bring her team to work together, and she felt like giving up. No matter what Loony Lav prophesied, her fate couldn't be written in the stars, because she'd run it into the ground.

Chapter 6.5

. . .

FRIDAY 4:02 PM

    The BOY Version: I noticed you bailed

    Willa: So

    The BOY Version: Smart to make a clean break

    Willa: What are you talking about?

    The BOY Version: Noticed your elf and vamp getting cozy
at the gazebo

    Willa: Don't.

    The BOY Version: For real, r u ok?

    Willa: Yes

    The BOY Version: You can do better

    Willa: Same

SATURDAY 10:52 AM

    Tarron: You up?

    Willa: Yep

    Tarron: Can you work on the project today?

    Willa: Nope

    Tarron: What's up?

    Willa: Work

    Tarron: I'll come by

    Willa: It would be better if you didn't

SUNDAY 1:16 PM

    Tarron: Want to grab some coffee?

3:27 PM **WILLA:** Sorry, lost track of time

    Willa: Check our Google folder, I got some work done

    Tarron: I thought we were going to work on it together

    Willa: I was on a roll

Tarron: Will I get to see you today?
Willa: I don't think it's a good idea
Tarron: Why not?
Willa: I had a heart-to-heart with my dad
Tarron: Everything ok?
Willa: There's no way you can understand
Willa: My dad asked me to give the pack another chance
Tarron: What does that even mean?
Willa: I'm torn
Tarron: What do you need from me?
Willa: Please, don't make me type it out
Tarron: . . .
Willa: Space, I just need some space

CHAPTER 7

*M*onday, Willa hated herself for walking past her Scooby gang and sitting with the Kasun pack. She'd promised her dad to give her brother and the others another chance. A chance to allow the bond connecting pack members to strengthen. But she felt her alliance with Tarron and the others fracture after she turned to face the opposite direction.

Tuesday, the ache in her soul to exchange a smile with Scarlet or Elle kept her focused on the speckled linoleum floor. In her classes, she buried her nose in her textbooks. In the hallways, shoulders pressed close, but she sensed herself growing emotionally distant.

Wednesday, she survived the day without saying one word out loud.

Thursday, she slept, ditching school. It wasn't until noon that she remembered her project with Tarron was due the following day. She pulled out her laptop and quickly opened up their shared files. Tarron hadn't opened them.

Willa wouldn't bail on the presentation or paper. He didn't deserve it. She started compiling the research she'd gathered and worked through points for the presentation. After organizing a slideshow, she scribbled out some thoughts on notecards. The notes served as an outline for the paper she typed and printed.

Before she knew it, her dad strode into their apartment. His broad frame, dark hair, and affinity for plaid made him look more like a lumberjack than a sheriff. He pulled off his jacket and hung it in the front closet. It only took four steps to reach her at the other side of the room, and he leaned over and kissed her forehead.

"You're up late. Homework?" he asked.

Pressing a thumb to her phone, she saw that it was after ten. "Yeah, a history presentation on an Archer's Banded Kettle Helm."

"Cool." Her dad plopped on the couch and stretched out, propping his boots on the coffee table. "Did you eat dinner?"

"I lost track of time." She clicked to save the file as she closed the window. "But now that you mention it, I'm starving."

"Pizza?" He guessed.

Willa shook her head.

"Hmm . . . Chinese?"

"Burgers?" Willa countered.

Her dad nodded his approval. "Want to take my truck? I'm beat."

"Sure," she answered with a grin. "The usual?"

"Yeah." He leaned his head back into the cushion and closed his eyes. It wasn't often Sheriff Ric Kasun let himself get caught in a vulnerable position, and in that moment, he seemed more peaceful than when he was armed and patrolling the town borders.

Willa had always thought peace and security went hand in hand, but her dad being relaxed and exposed had brought him the most peace. Being able to let go of the outside world and the expectations that went with it, allowing himself to be comfortable.

"Dad, can I ask you something?"

"Sure, but if it's about helmets or archers, I'm not sure I'll be much help," he said with a smirk.

Willa moved to plop down beside him. "You want to keep me safe," she said, feeling so small next to him.

"Yes, it's my job as your father, as your acting alpha, and as the town's sheriff. Why?" He peeked through one eyelid.

Willa shifted uncomfortably. "What if I don't become alpha, and the Novaks replace you?"

"Ana Novak becoming alpha may seem like the end of the world, but we'll survive. The Kasuns have made it through much worse. Plus, Ana is young. Her father and the Court won't allow her to make major decisions on her own for years," he explained.

"But what if they replace you as sheriff, too?"

Ric closed his eyes for a moment, processing the notion. "Honestly, I hadn't thought about it. The Court appointed me as sheriff, and I'm not sure the Novaks could make that kind of call."

"Well, I've been taking your advice. Hanging out with Kase and the others more." She winced. "And, I know it was meant to help me fit in and protect me, but—"

"But you're miserable?"

"Yeah." She frowned. "I've been managing to keep myself together, but the tighter I try to hold on, the more out of control I feel. And, I don't want to let you down."

"Come here." He shifted to his side and wrapped his arms around his baby girl. "There's miserable, and then there's miserable. You have to ask yourself which is worse—the way the pack makes you feel when you're with them or the way they treat you when you're hanging out with your new friends. Once you decide which miserable you can live with, you'll know how to move forward."

"Would you be mad if I chose an elf, witch, vampire, and dragon shifter over the pack?" she asked.

Her dad laid his head against hers. "I'm not sure that's what you're doing. Your mom would say you're adding to your pack, and while there is a Novak or two that don't deserve it, I believe you'd risk your life for any of ours."

"No pressure." She pushed against his chest teasingly, but not so hard that he'd loosen his embrace. It felt like home to be in her daddy's arms. Not because he held her captive, but because he was beginning to let go.

"How about I make you a PB&J? Then we don't have to leave, and we can try to catch a late-night lip sync battle."

"Sounds perfect," she agreed with a smile.

In bed by midnight, Willa lay under a mound of blankets looking beyond her window at the moon. Its power filled her. It felt like the joy overflowing from the time she spent with her dad. Willa wouldn't go another day without talking to Tarron, Scarlet, Elle, and even Bale. It took some time to find sleep, but when she did, a weight had been lifted, and she felt a peace about her decision.

A morning freeze had frosted every window pane in the apartment, blocking the morning light. Willa woke up with a jolt, immediately worried she would be late. Reaching over to her phone, she tilted it, only to see that she'd woken up twenty-four minutes early. Perfect. She had time to pick up coffee.

Arriving at Havenwood Falls High early, with her Americano and an extra hot cinnamon latte for Tarron, Willa stood on the front steps at the entrance. She hoped to catch Tarron so they could go over their project before class, not to mention so she could apologize.

Tarron had given her space, just like she'd asked. He hadn't stopped by her locker or visited her at work. In that moment, as students rushed into the building before the first bell, Willa wished Tarron stood directly in front of her. But he never arrived.

She wouldn't blame him for bailing.

Willa turned and tossed the two drinks in a nearby trash can. Tugging on her backpack's shoulder straps, she took the steps two at a time and mentally prepared to give the presentation on her own.

Just like the second day of school, Willa stopped short of the back section the pack sat in and took a seat in the middle of the room. When the final bell rang, every desk was occupied except the one next to her. Ms. Bast had worn her hair down, and as she turned her back to the students, her dark curls obstructed Willa's view of the names she started writing on the board.

"Psst!" Someone called from behind Willa.

She looked over her shoulder, and everyone looked busy, pulling their papers out of their backpacks or reading over notes for their presentations. She turned back around and did the same.

"Psst!"

Willa wanted to ignore the noise, but it sounded familiar. She turned one more time, and her brother leaned forward in his desk with his eyebrows raised.

"Are you going to be okay if Tarron doesn't show?" he asked.

Ana's eyes darted up at the elf's name.

"I'll be fine." Willa waved her brother's worry for her away. "It's not like I didn't bail on him all week."

Ana rolled her eyes. "We'll just tell Ms. Bast that Santa's helper wasn't very helpful. She'll totes understand, and hopefully you'll never have to mutt-it-up again."

"What did you just—" Willa pushed up from her desk, but Ms. Bast's knuckles rapped on the white board and forced her back to her seat.

"The order of the presentations is listed, and I expect everyone to show respect for their classmates." Ms. Bast moved to stand in front of Willa's row. "You will all be graded on peer reviews as well as your presentations, so take a worksheet and pass them back."

After divvying up the papers, Ms. Bast walked to the empty desk next to Willa. She sat and called up the first pair. Willa attempted calming herself by perusing the list, but found her name at the bottom. She pulled on the pendant of her necklace, hating the anticipation of having to go last.

Ms. Bast leaned toward Willa and whispered, "Tarron asked if your presentation could be the finale."

The request had to mean he'd show, but how did he get out of having to sit through everyone else's project? Willa wanted to take a nap during Maria and Joseph's list of facts, then Kase and Elle presented. The two did a thorough job describing a steel helmet from the Renaissance shaped like a lion's head. They even had the class laughing when they compared it to other helmets worn in in the same period shaped like animal heads.

A few other students gave entertaining presentations, including Ana and Ivan, as much as Willa hated to admit it. Her favorite had to be Scarlet and Bale's take on modern masks and makeup used for disguises. Willa slowly became aware of the masks she and her friends wore on a daily basis. Camouflaging themselves among their own kind, covering up their fear with fake smiles, and obscuring their curiosity with insults were all ways to fit in, hide, and protect themselves.

Then the room grew silent, waiting for her to take her turn, without Tarron.

She walked up to the front of the room, her eyes darting around like she'd find him somewhere hiding behind a bookshelf or desk. Taking her time, she plugged her thumb drive into the computer on Ms. Bast's desk. A few whispers distracted her, and when she glanced over her shoulder, a glint of metal caught her eye.

Tarron had entered the room in full costume.

A flat, open-sided silver helm pushed down his hair, and a leather breastplate covered his chest. He held a longbow at his side and arrow feathers peeked from behind his shoulder, strapped to his back in a quiver. A sword hung from his belt, and he wore brown pants and boots. There were extra touches to the costume Willa noticed, as they were a part of her research.

Willa tilted her head, curious about where he was going with this stunt. Tarron grinned. He showed up. He hadn't planned on letting her fail. A wave of emotion built up in her chest, making her want to apologize to him in front of the class.

Then Ms. Bast cleared her throat.

"As promised." Tarron bowed toward the teacher.

Ms. Bast nodded with a smile. "Just remember, weapons are not allowed on campus. It doesn't matter if it's a personal collection or plastic props, you have to leave directly after your presentation and get all of that off the school property." She waved up and down at his costume. "Or the principal will be torturing both of us."

"Yes, ma'am."

Willa pulled up the presentation she'd prepared, and with the first slide, introduced herself and her partner. During their lesson on the kettle helmet, she described how the helm and other armor was worn through history while Tarron gave a quick demonstration. Students laughed as Tarron modeled each piece of his armor. He'd brought an apple, and while she hoped to place it on top of Ana's big blue bow, he set it on top of a bookshelf at the back of the room. Gasps filled the room when the fruit was pierced by an arrow.

Everyone had been enraptured by them, well, everyone except Ana. She sat with her arms crossed and frowned through every slide.

To bring the presentation to a close, Willa added, "The kettle helmet was worn mainly by infantry, or foot soldiers. En masse, with matching armor, they all appeared to be identical, but many of the soldiers were ripped from their own lives and forced to fight for causes that weren't their own. I don't know about you, but I'm glad I don't *have* to hide or push someone else's agenda. I have the power to fight my own battles."

When they finished, the class clapped, and Willa retrieved her thumb drive. As she turned to walk back to her desk, Tarron exited the room. She looked from her empty chair to the doorway and decided to go with her gut. She walked out after him.

"Hey!" she called. "Tarron, wait up!"

He turned the corner, and Willa almost stopped when he didn't hear her. But, an urgency inside quickened her pace.

"Please, stop!" she hollered, not caring who heard her. "I'm sorry, please hear me out!"

As she reached the end of the hallway, she turned to follow Tarron and collided with a leather breastplate. She shook her head and looked up at a grinning elf. He had waited.

CHAPTER 8

*O*n the one hand, everyone got enough sleep the previous night to take on the ACTs. On the other, most of the junior class moped into the high school cafeteria, depressed after losing last night's football game. The team had proved less successful than in seasons past, having only won three of their six games. Morale was low, and four hours with a number two pencil wasn't going to help.

For the last week, Willa, Tarron, Elle, Scarlet, and Bale had spent every evening going through a set of notecards Scarlet put together to study. Everyone else at Havenwood Falls High School had been consumed with football. Kase and his buddies rallied at their lunch table every day leading up to the big game. If they'd won, the blue and silver Dragons would have been a wild card team in the playoffs the next weekend. There hadn't been a season in four years that the team didn't cross over into the basketball season.

Thanks to their loss, this year's homecoming would feel less like a ticker tape parade to celebrate a group of guys who won their version of the Super Bowl, and more like a dance. Willa was torn between ignoring the tradition and asking Tarron if he wanted to go with her. The more time she spent with Tarron, the more she knew not inviting him would be a cop out.

"Good morning," Scarlet greeted. Her wide smile and the bounce in her step as she met Willa wasn't typical Scarlet behavior.

Willa was the first to arrive in the transformed space. The tables had been folded and rolled to the far end of the cafeteria. In their place, over a hundred desks filled the room. The public high school served as the host for today's test. If Willa didn't make a great score, she could take it again when Sun and Moon Academy, the private school, hosted. She wasn't surprised when she didn't recognize a few of the teens trickling into the empty seats.

"Morning," Willa answered. "You seem wide awake. What kind of coffee did you order?"

"I drink tea, and you know that." Scarlet took a seat at a desk and patted the chair next to her. "I need to talk. Girl talk."

Willa's eyebrows pulled up behind her dark bangs. "I'm a girl. But, are you expecting me to talk or listen?"

"Listen."

Willa swiped her thumb and finger across her lips and twisted them like she was locking them shut.

"Bale asked me to homecoming," Scarlet started and stopped. She didn't say anything else.

Willa waited.

More students began to fill empty seats, and Willa looked down at her watch. They had fifteen minutes before the test began, and she knew the rest of their Scooby gang would arrive soon. She needed to speed this girl talk along.

"So, what did you say?" she asked.

Scarlet fidgeted with one of her long red braids. "That's the thing. I stuttered a yes, then said something about how all of us could have dinner and make a night of it. His whole demeanor changed. I think he was asking me out, and I ruined it."

Willa felt bad for Scarlet, but she also felt a twinge of jealousy. "I'm sure we can fix this."

"You think so?" Scarlet's voice was hopeful.

Willa rubbed her chin. "I know so. But I need the truth. Do you want to go with Bale alone or do you want to all go together but as couples?"

"I'm not saying we can't all hang out, but I think I want it to be the two of us," she admitted.

As Tarron entered the cafeteria, with Bale and Elle close behind, Willa leaned over and whispered, "Okay, I can work with that."

"Hey guys!" Scarlet waved the others over.

"Are you two ready for this?" Tarron asked.

Willa noticed Bale take the chair farthest away from Scarlet and avoid eye contact. Elle took the seat on the other side of Scarlet, and Tarron sat in the seat next to Willa. He nudged her for an answer.

"I even sharpened an extra pencil." Willa waved her writing utensils in the air. "What's everyone doing after the test?"

"I don't have anything planned," Tarron answered first, then Bale shrugged.

"Hanging out?" Scarlet asked.

"Yeah." Willa glanced at Elle to make sure she felt included. "How about everyone come over to my place this afternoon for a movie marathon?"

Elle picked at her nails. "Are you sure?"

"Of course," she answered.

"Everyone, take your seats!" Ms. Bast's voice echoed from a table buried by stacks of paper.

Willa understood why Elle might have reservations about coming to her house. Any vampire would want to avoid an encounter with a pack of werewolves in the woods. She would feel the same way about walking into a nest of vamps. Willa probably needed to clarify that she lived above the family's store.

A group of teachers fanned out through the room, checking

everyone's pencils. Ms. Bast placed red-rimmed glasses on the tip of her nose and read over the instructions while the tests were passed out, and Willa pushed thoughts of homecoming and dating and dresses to the back of her mind. Willa wasn't sure what her college plans were yet, but she hoped her test score would allow her to keep her options open.

"Break the seal and begin," Ms. Bast directed and scanned the room with her black eyes.

Willa flew through English and reading, and when she finished before her friends, she enjoyed peeking over at Tarron. He had the cutest way of tapping the end of his pencil against the tip of his nose while he read. Science kept Willa second-guessing herself, and the math section made her want to stab herself in the ear.

Just before they began the writing portion, Tarron leaned over and whispered, "Relax, the hardest part is over for you."

"You'll do fine," she assured him.

Ms. Bast cleared her throat to get everyone's attention. "You may start."

Earlier that week, they'd all agreed to meet in the school parking lot to discuss how they did. One by one, they each turned in their tests and walked out into the brisk fall afternoon. Bale had been the first one out of the cafeteria, and Scarlet walked out last.

"How do you think you did?" Willa asked her.

Scarlet pulled gloves out of her jacket pocket and fitted them over her hands. "Terrible. I completely froze on the writing and didn't finish."

"I bet you did great." Elle consoled her. "I didn't finish the science."

Scarlet zipped up her jacket and started to walk over to her vintage VW Golf. "Let's talk about it at Willa's. I'm freezing!"

"Okay, girls in Scarlet's car, and boys can meet us there," Willa suggested.

Bale and Tarron nodded their approval and jumped into the

Corvette. Willa offered the front seat in Scarlet's car to Elle and slid into the backseat of the witch's silver hatchback. Once inside, and clear of being heard by the guys, Willa explained to Elle that she lived in the town square over the store and not in the forest with the rest of the Kasun pack.

Elle pressed her lips together, trying to restrain herself.

"Go ahead." Willa kneed the back of the passenger seat. "Say whatever is on your mind before you explode."

Elle hadn't been around other supernaturals before her family moved to town, so she observed everything. It seemed to be her way of getting to know all of them without sticking her foot in her mouth. The first week they met, she'd asked Tarron if Puck from *A Midsummer Night's Dream* was real, and if his family knew Shakespeare.

"The Kasun pack, your family, lives east of Havenwood Heights, in the forest . . ."

"Yes," Willa confirmed, "in cabins. It's a small community, but it allows them to shift without having to worry about being seen."

Relief flashed across her face as she pressed her lips together and nodded. "Okay. I mean, good. It's just that, I didn't know if, er, I wanted to make sure I wouldn't wake up to—"

"A wolf encounter?" Willa asked.

Pink blotches spread up Elle's neck to her cheeks. "Sure, um, yes."

Scarlet pulled out of the parking lot, onto Main Street. "Now that we've settled the Kasun sleeping arrangements, can we please address how I'm going to clear things up with Bale? He's been avoiding me all morning."

"I noticed that, too. What happened?" Elle asked, eager to change the topic.

"I fumbled up my words, and now he'll never go to homecoming with me," Scarlet wailed. She leaned forward, and as they slowed to a four-way stop, she banged her head against the steering wheel.

"You could not have fumbled any worse than my brother at last night's game," Willa joked, but neither of the girls laughed.

Elle suddenly lit up with excitement. "You need to do one of those prom-posal things!"

"But it's homecoming," Scarlet argued.

Willa stuck her head between their two seats. "I agree with Elle. You need to let Bale know he's not just a friend like the rest of us."

"Pot calling the kettle black much?" Scarlet teased, and this time Elle giggled, but Willa wasn't in the mood.

She still liked Tarron—really liked him. She felt like she should try to accept that he only wanted to be friends. Willa didn't blame him. If Scarlet and Bale went to next week's dance as a couple, maybe she and Tarron could still go as friends with Elle. The problem was the theme required everyone to dress up as famous couples.

Willa leaned back in her seat and sank down a bit before responding. "Fine. I like him, but I messed it up when I asked for space. I'm a chicken for not bringing it up. But I bet he doesn't want anything more than friendship, and if that's all I can get, I'll take it. Anyways, we need to focus on fixing your problem."

Elle turned to face Willa. "What if you ask him?"

"I bet he'd say yes!" Scarlet encouraged.

"I don't know." Willa shook her head. "I'd rather not mess things up with him any more than I already have. Plus, if I don't ask him, the three of us can go together."

"Oh, well, I won't be here." Elle turned back around, avoiding eye contact.

"What?" Scarlet's mouth hung open.

"Yeah, my family has to go out of town for a few days. We'll be back by Sunday night, but my mom has already called the school office and gotten my Friday absence excused."

Scarlet pulled into the town square and parked in front of Backwoods Sport & Ski, next to Tarron's car. The guys weren't waiting for them, so Willa examined the sidewalk. Shoppers walked in and out of the stores and restaurants, but she noticed a few of them pointing to the center of the square.

Willa opened her door and stepped out. As she turned to see which quirky town event she forgot about, she watched as a crowd of people surrounded the gazebo. The people moved around the fountain at the center of the quad and pushed up on their toes for a better look.

"What do you guys think is going on over there?" Willa asked.

Scarlet and Elle made eye contact over the top of the car, and Willa picked up on a knowing exchange between them.

"Let's go see." Elle hooked her arm with Willa and pulled her across the street.

Scarlet followed and caught up to Willa's other side and whispered, "Don't be mad at me."

Willa's brow furrowed. The closer they came to the gazebo, the less she could see. Sparkling twinkle lights draped from the ceiling covering the platform, and thumping dance music drifted over the growing crowd.

"Excuse me," Elle said. The young couple in front of them turned and scooted over.

Scarlet tapped on a young girl's shoulder. "Pardon us."

As she slid to the side and let them by, Willa's brother Tate came into view. He didn't have his cadet uniform on, but wore the store's standard work uniform—jeans and a Backwoods Sport & Ski long-sleeved T-shirt. He was supposed to be covering for her while she took her ACTs.

"Tate? What are you—"

Tate pivoted to let her by, and she noticed two things immediately. First, Tate hadn't smiled that widely in a long time. Second, Tarron stood in the middle of the gazebo. Large silver stars hung around his head, and he held one in his hands.

"Go on," Scarlet said.

With a nudge, Willa took the first few steps. She realized the stars, fluttering in the afternoon breeze, were signs with words written on them.

She started to make out her name written on a star, then her eyes darted to read them all.

Willa & Tarron
Written
in the
Stars

Willa covered her mouth with her hands. She finally met Tarron's eyes, and he lifted the star he held to cover his face.

Will you be my date to homecoming?

"Yes!"

~

Chapter 8.5

SUNDAY 11:43 AM

The BOY Version: Tate told me that you're going to homecoming

Willa: And

The BOY Version: Are you sure about him?

Willa: More sure than I am of you

The BOY Version: Ouch!

Willa: Be honest, you're more worried I'll make you look bad

The BOY Version: I really am just looking out for you

Willa: He makes me happy

The BOY Version: Then I'll try harder to get on board

Willa: You do that

The BOY Version: Same

Willa: But does she really make you happy?

The BOY Version: . . .

· · ·

SUNDAY 3:22 PM

Scarlet: BTW, Bale and I straightened everything out
Willa: When?
Scarlet: He walked me home when we left your place
Willa: Since the theme requires a costume this year, who are you guys coming as?
Scarlet: He joked about dressing up as Astrid & Stormfly
Willa: How to train your dragon? Bwahaha!
Scarlet: Yeah, I think he just wants to see if I'll dress up like a Viking
Willa: Good luck with that!

SUNDAY 7:56 PM

Willa: What have you been up to today?
Tarron: Bale wants to show up to homecoming shifted
Willa: I heard
Tarron: Who do you want to dress up as?
Willa: Shakespeare is too obvious
Tarron: Probably
Tarron: And you won't get me in tights
Willa: I just got a mental image
Tarron: Sorry
Willa: LOL
Tarron: How about Gatsby & Daisy?
Willa: Meh
Willa: I'd almost rather go as us...but with a happily ever after
Tarron: I'm down for that
Willa: And if anyone asks we can say we're Winston and Julia from 1984
Tarron: I'll have to look that one up
Willa: Really?

Tarron: . . .

Willa: How can I call you my boyfriend if you haven't read Orwell?

Tarron: Boyfriend?

Willa: . . .

Tarron: I like the way that sounds

Willa: Then you better start reading

CHAPTER 9

*W*illa walked home after school on Friday, with Tarron close at her side. He'd offered her a ride, but she enjoyed the colder temperatures. She told him it was silly to walk her home, then walk back to the school to retrieve his car, but he insisted.

The week had been less hectic with football season over and the ACTs taken. Willa spent the afternoons with Tarron and their friends. She'd memorized all their favorite drinks at Coffee Haven and favorite pizza toppings at Napoli's. She didn't think things could get any better. Then, Tarron kissed her goodbye and promised to pick her up by 6:30.

Scarlet had planned to get ready at Willa's apartment and would be arriving soon. While Willa waited, she pulled out her dress and shoes, laying them out on her bed. The sweetheart neckline and shorter length would normally be worn in the summer, but Willa had a vintage motorcycle jacket she'd wear over it and studded high tops.

At the sound of knocking, Willa ran to the door and invited her friend inside. One of Scarlet's arms had a hanging bag draped across it, and the other held a tote stuffed with her heels and styling products. Willa grabbed her dress and waved Scarlet inside.

"This is going to be fun." Scarlet bounced inside.

"Yeah." Willa set the garment bag on her bed next to her dress. "I hate that Elle couldn't make it. Do you know what her weekend out of town was all about?"

"No idea." She hung her tote on a hook on the back of Willa's bedroom door. "I wouldn't blame her if she made the whole thing up to get out of going without a date. Not that she would do that!"

"I'm going to text her, and make sure she knows we miss her."

"Good idea." Scarlet unzipped the bag her dress hung in, and what she pulled out surprised Willa.

"No. Way." Willa giggled. The red flowy wrap dress draped to the floor, dramatic but also simple, almost identical to the one worn in *The Princess Bride*. The movie was one of Willa's favorites, and immediately Willa knew who Scarlet and Bale would be impersonating.

Scarlet wrapped her arm around the fabric, pressing it against her stomach. "You don't think it's lame?"

"No! It's brilliant! And, I can't imagine Bale in anything but a black outfit. Which one of you thought of it?"

Scarlet rolled her eyes. "I did, but only after he suggested characters from Game of Thrones. Come on, let's get changed. I want to see that on you." Scarlet pointed to Willa's dress on the bed.

"As you wish," Willa said with a laugh.

The two girls changed and helped each other with their hair and make-up. Neither one of them went overboard, but their costumes didn't call for heavy eye liner or thickly layered red lipstick. Scarlet pulled a few locks of hair back loosely, but left the rest down and wavy. Willa tucked a clip with sparkling amethysts in her hair. The light purple added to the concept she and Tarron had come up with for their costumes.

A buzz pulled Willa away from the mirror, and her phone screen lit up with a message from Tarron. He planned to pick her up in fifteen minutes. They wouldn't all be going to the dance together, because Scarlet wanted to make sure Bale understood they were on a date. The dragon's bruised ego needed a boost, and Willa didn't mind the idea of some extra time alone with Tarron.

He hadn't held her hand or tried to kiss her since before she'd asked for space, and she was hoping they could fix that tonight. Willa swiped to check the time on her phone.

The front door of the apartment opened and closed, making Willa's heart stop. Had Tarron arrived early?

"Willa?" Her dad called from the living room. "Is it safe for me to enter?"

Willa looked over at Scarlet, who shrugged and turned back to smooth out her dress with flat hands against her hips.

"Yeah, we're decent."

"We?" he asked and stepped into her bedroom. He took in the clothes strewn on the floor and bags opened on the bed, then he noticed Scarlet standing in front of the mirror. "Miss Howe, right?"

"Yes, sir. Scarlet. It's nice to meet you." She stepped forward and stuck her hand out for him to shake.

He smiled and replied, "It's nice to meet you, too. Princess Buttercup?"

"Yes, sir."

He grinned and waved her formality away. "Please, call me Ric."

"The theme is Written in the Stars this year, so we're all dressed as famous couples," Willa explained.

"Ahh." He inspected his daughter's black cocktail dress with a cosmic print wrapped around her waist and glinting stars intricately placed on the bodice. "Then who are you going as?"

"I'm going as the stars, but you'll have to wait to see Tarron's costume."

Ric's head tilted, confused.

"At first he wanted to go as an astronaut, but I convinced him the suit would be too difficult to work around in the bathroom."

Ric chuckled. "I'm sure he just wants to impress you. I love that you're wearing your mother's stone." He leaned forward and kissed her cheek.

Willa placed her fingers over her necklace. "Thank you." She pushed up on her toes and gave her father a kiss on the cheek. "You know, I figured everyone would be showing up as—"

"Romeo and Juliet?" Her dad interrupted. "Your brother fell into that trap."

Scarlet let out a laugh from the bathroom, and Willa and her dad joined in.

Their laughing abruptly ceased at the sound of three raps on the door.

Scarlet jumped. "I bet that's Bale." She moved into the bedroom and started throwing all her things into her bag.

"Don't worry about your stuff." Willa put a hand on her arm to stop her. "You can come by later and grab it."

Ric had already started for the door.

"You'll want to be ready to leave before my dad interrogates Bale."

Scarlet gave herself one more once-over in the mirror and walked into the living room. Willa stepped into the doorway, and she couldn't believe how perfect Bale's costume looked. From the black mask to the sword to the boots, Bale had captured Westley in his Dread Pirate Roberts outfit. The only difference was the dark hair that escaped his mask.

Whatever her dad was asking him, Bale froze at the sight of Scarlet. "You look amazing."

"Thank you." Scarlet blushed.

"Sheriff Kasun, we have a stop to make before we head to the dance. Did you have anything else you wanted to add?" Bale asked, his smile faltering.

Willa understood the feeling. Her dad was intimidating. But he was also a great dad, and she figured he knew that Scarlet didn't have a father figure to instill fear in her dates.

"Just make sure she has a wonderful time." Ric narrowed his eyes at Bale.

Bale nodded. "Of course." He reached out a hand toward Scarlet, and she took it.

As they exited, Scarlet glanced over her shoulder and mouthed thank you to Willa's dad. She waved at Willa and said, "We'll see you and Tarron at the dance."

"Or now," Tarron's voice echoed down the hall. "Hey guys, you both look great."

Tarron passed Scarlet and Bale and stopped in the doorway. His mouth fell open at the sight of Willa. Ric stepped into view, and he quickly pulled himself together and shoved his hands in the pockets of his black suit pants. Underneath his jacket, Willa made out the image on his T-shirt. She hoped everyone would get the reference they were trying to make. Her dad would be the test run.

"Would you like to come in?" Ric asked.

"Thank you." Tarron stepped into the living room and slid his jacket off his shoulders. The black T-shirt he wore had an image of the moon printed on the front. His white suspenders were a surprise to Willa, but she liked them.

"So, what are your plans with Willa this evening?" Ric asked.

One of Tarron's eyebrows lifted. "I was hoping to keep it a surprise—"

Ric's chest rumbled, and Willa giggled. "Dad, give it a rest. Did you ask Kase what his plans with Ana were?"

"No, but—"

Willa laid a hand on her father's arm. "Would you feel better if I gave you Tarron's cell number? That way the surprise isn't ruined, but you can trace his phone."

"I wouldn't—well, unless it got really late." Ric corrected himself with a grin.

"I'll text it to you."

Ric's jaw flexed. "What time do you think you'll be home?"

Willa looked up to Tarron.

"The dance is over at eleven, but I'd like to keep her out until midnight." He hadn't asked a question, but raised his eyebrows like he needed permission. "If that's okay with you, sir?"

"Midnight." Ric held his hand out to shake on it.

"Thank you."

Ric tightened his grip. "Don't thank me yet. You lose the right to take her out again if you're late. Or if you harm one hair on her head—or her heart."

"Okay, Dad, you can let him go now," Willa assured.

Ric let Tarron go, and the elf shook out his fingers.

"See you later, sweetheart." Ric waved goodbye as they left. As Willa reached for her key, he said, "Don't worry about that. I'll be up."

Willa giggled as she grabbed her vintage leather jacket instead. "Goodnight, Dad."

She and Tarron made their way down the stairs and out the building's back door. The last thing she wanted to do was parade through the store all dressed up. At least wearing studded black high tops, she didn't have to worry about tripping and wobbling on heels all night.

"So, your dad is funny." Tarron smiled as he held the passenger side door open for her.

Willa slipped into the Corvette. "That's one way to put it. He actually mentioned his concealed handgun last year when Joseph Greg asked me out." Her face soured at the thought.

"What? You didn't want him to be the moon to your stars?" Tarron asked, referencing their costumes, as he revved the engine.

"Don't you remember that freshmen hazing you guys went through on the football team? I've seen Joseph's full moon."

The two laughed, and Willa watched as Tarron focused on a

few turns and some oncoming traffic. She really liked being with him. He didn't like her because she could be the next alpha or dislike her because she couldn't shift. He hadn't been scared away by her brothers, and he gave her space when she needed it.

"What's wrong with you?" she blurted.

Tarron glanced at her, but quickly moved his eyes back to the road. "Ummm . . . where to begin? I always miss the hamper when I try to toss my dirty clothes in it, and I rarely pick them up off the floor. My mom says I spend too much time playing video games. My dad is always pestering me about work—"

"Tarron, really, is that all you've got?"

The car slowed down, and Willa looked out her window. Tarron had driven them as far on Main Street as they could go, to Danzan Park. They pulled over on the other side of Bels Creek. As he shut the car off, the headlights faded, and Willa could only see a few feet past the hood. She didn't have the ability to see in the dark like her werewolf family. Even Kase only had it when in his wolf form.

"What are we doing out here?" Willa asked.

"Surprise, remember?" Tarron jumped out of the car and reached for a basket and blanket in the trunk.

Tarron spread the blanket along the bank of the creek and opened the basket. He pulled a lantern out first and lit up a small area around them. The peaceful sound of water running toward Mathews River and the thousands of stars beaming above them made the setting perfect.

"Are you going to be cold? I have another blanket—"

"I'm good." She moved to peek in the basket. "What else is in there?"

"Food."

"What kind of food?"

Tarron paused above the basket and looked at the blanket. "Can we sit first? I want to tell you something, but I'm not sure I want to hand you something you can throw at me first."

"Okay . . ." Willa tilted her head. "Is it serious?"

84

"Kind of. It might be something you'd categorize as wrong with me." He sat on the blanket, his legs remaining straight in front of him, and patted the space next to him.

"I'm all ears." She smiled reassuringly and placed her hand next to his so that they brushed against each other.

"I quit the football team because I have the ability to convince or manipulate other people to do what I want. The power didn't fully develop until our sophomore year, and my mom thinks that my witch side amplifies my elfin abilities when my emotions are heightened."

"That's crazy, but why would that be something wrong? I mean, you recognized it and dropped out of football. If anything, you should think I'm a horrible person for not telling anyone about my abilities."

Tarron shook his head. "I don't think you understand, Willa. When we first met, I was so worried I'd say or do something that would cause you to like me more than you would have if I didn't have this power. I have to be so careful, especially with humans."

"I can't remember ever feeling like you influenced me. I mean, you may have used your mystical power to get me to try that disgusting strawberry shake at the Burger Bar." She nudged him with her elbow.

Tarron sat up and crossed his legs in front of him. "I never want to influence you to do anything you don't want to do. When you told me you needed space, I realized my abilities didn't work on you. At least not as strongly as they had with others. I just need to tell you before things get serious—I mean—"

Willa's mouth spread into a wide smile. He planned for things to get serious. Instead of being scared or nervous, she welcomed the stir of emotions in her stomach. She leaned forward slightly and took in his features. His white hair, messy as always, made him appear wild and mischievous. His light eyes and freckles gave him a boyish charm, but his full lips and jawline made her want to lean in closer and kiss him.

"Are you doing it right now?" she asked.

He whispered, "Doing what?"

"Making me want to kiss you?"

"I'd have to say it out loud." He grinned. "Plus, I told you, it doesn't work on you."

She leaned forward and brushed her lips softly over his, testing his response. Tarron's eyes searched hers.

"Are you sure?" she teased and kissed him again.

CHAPTER 10

*T*arron and Willa entered the high school gym looking like they could be a centerpiece on one of the tables. Black paper and giant silver stars hung from the ceiling. Lights twinkled along the walls. A stage had been set up under one of the basketball hoops and a space cleared in front of it for dancing. The area was surrounded by tables covered in black tablecloths and glitter.

The tables and refreshments were swarming with students, but the dance floor remained empty. The music lilted through the air, not exactly romantic or energizing. Willa had been dreading dancing with Tarron. She looked down at his black boots and hoped he had plenty of polish at home, because she had a feeling she'd be scuffing them up.

"Do you want something to drink?" Tarron asked.

Willa glanced around the room in search of Scarlet. "Sure." She pointed to a red dress at a table toward the back of the gym. "I'll head over to meet Scarlet and Bale."

"Any food?" he asked before walking away.

Willa pushed up on her toes to kiss him on the cheek. "Thank you, but I don't think I can eat another bite. Maybe later, if we dance off some of the burgers."

Tarron had made an effort to recreate their first date, without actually going to the drive-in. After eating, they went for a walk and lost track of time. It had been easy to leave the town on the other side of the creek.

"Hey, you two," Willa greeted Bale and Scarlet. They'd both sat down at a table, with their chairs so close their shoulders touched. Willa grinned at their affection. "Where did you take Scarlet for dinner?"

"Oh, well—"

"He cooked for me!" Scarlet's face lit up. She wrapped her arm around his and squeezed. "It was the best steak I've ever eaten."

"You cook?" Willa's eyes widened in wonder.

"I grill. There's a big difference," he corrected, then rubbed his hand over his mouth and mumbled, "And, my mom shmunted-a-mean-squirrel."

Willa's nose wrinkled up in question.

"His mom wanted to meet Scarlet," Tarron clarified as he sat down next to her. He set a plastic cup filled with blue liquid in front of her. "I had to meet her, too, before I could take Bale out." He laughed.

"Shut up, man. She's protective." He leaned forward. "And you don't want to make a dragon shifter angry, especially a mother."

"I bet my dad could give her a run for her money," Willa said.

"Nah, your dad's intimidating, but imagine him shifting to the size of a school bus and breathing fire because you're out past curfew."

Willa looked to Tarron and Scarlet, who both shrugged. She'd actually like to see Bale's mom shift. Some nights, she looked up to the sky to try to find one of the dragons flying overhead. A few of them worked with her father and patrolled the skies, but she'd only seen the shadow of one gliding above at night.

A group of students barged into the gym in a commotion, and Willa immediately recognized Ana's whiny voice. "This is not music. It's elevator crap. Someone tell that DJ we aren't paying him to be put to sleep."

Scarlet giggled and whispered to the rest of them, "I wish someone would put her to sleep."

They all laughed, but Ana and Scarlet both had a point. The music needed to change, and someone needed to put Ana in her place. Willa could at least do something about one of their problems.

"I'll be right back." She stood up and walked over to the stage. Marching up the steps near the DJ's booth, Willa slid behind a set of speakers in search of the person in charge.

A woman in ripped jeans and a crop top was stooped over on her cell phone. She had her phone against one ear and a finger in the other. Willa patted her arm to get her attention, and she jumped. The woman yelled something into the phone and hung up. She cocked an ear upward and frowned.

"What the—"

"Can I make a request?" Willa asked.

"Sure! Anything would be better than this." She moved to open her laptop, cords protruding from one side. "I asked your principal to click the Havenwood Falls High homecoming playlist, but it sounds like he chose the list at the top of my screen, Assisted Living Bingo Night. What do you wanna hear?"

"How about some Sylvan Esso or The Wombats?"

"Done and done," the DJ's hot pink lips exaggerated. "Have fun, honey!" she yelled over the song's beginning.

The fresh tempo called to the students lingering around the outer edges of the dance floor. As Willa made her way off the stage, she saw Tarron, Bale, and Scarlet move to meet her. Taking her hand, Tarron winked at her and pulled her behind him to the middle of the crowd.

By the fourth song, Willa was thankful she'd worn her high tops. A small pile of heels had amassed at the foot of the stage.

KALLIE ROSS

The beat of the music bounced off the walls of the gym and vibrated through Willa's chest. As the music slowed, a few loners cleared the area, but most of the couples gravitated together.

Tarron relaxed his arms around Willa's waist and leaned close to her ear. "Are you having fun?"

She smiled. "I never thought I'd have this much fun at a school dance. I feel so cliché."

"It's because we're here together." He squeezed Willa gently.

"Awww," Ana cooed. She wore a long gown, revealing a generous amount of cleavage, and her hair had been braided and piled on top of her head. She'd pulled away from Kase, and her face contorted. "You two are sickeningly sweet."

"Ana, not here," Kase warned. "Someone spiked the punch, and she's had three cups so far." He turned and tried to explain away her horrible behavior.

"Whoa!" Ana put her hands up in mock surrender. "You have about as much control over me as she does."

"Please, Ana, let's get you some fresh air," Kase coaxed. He settled a hand on the small of her back and attempted to gently pull her away.

The downbeat of the music boomed faster, and some of the seniors ran through the crowd causing a ruckus with a machete prop. Distracted, Willa glanced at the stage where Serena stood, Logan at her side.

A surge of heat burned Willa's chest, and she caught a glimpse of her pendant glowing under her chin. The wave of magic emanating from her seemed to have a similar effect on several supernaturals in the room. She saw Scarlet place a hand over one of her bracelets, and a guy shake his ring-clad hand in the air.

Suddenly, the chain at Willa's neck pulled, yanking her head forward. Clattering sounds echoed in the gym, along with a few ouches and gasps. Her pendant hovered an inch over her chest, and with a jerk, the chain snapped. Willa yelped as her mother's stone skittered out of sight.

Ana, eyes wide in astonishment, hurtled out of Kase's reach and tried to stop herself by flailing her arms in front of her. She fell on her face when Willa stepped out of the way.

"The necklace!" Ana frantically searched between heels and loafers and boots. Her teeth gritted together in a sneer at Willa.

Scarlet and Bale moved protectively to stand next to Willa.

Ana pushed herself up and looked Willa up and down. "It won't matter. Everything is set in motion, and that hideous thing can't save you now."

"Ana!" Kase took a step away from her, toward his sister. "What is wrong with you?"

"Wrong with me?" Ana got to her feet and pointed at Willa. "If there's anything wrong with anyone, it's her. She can't shift, she moved out of her house, she cut all her hair off just to avoid wearing a bow, and she's dating that—"

A growl stirred in Willa's, Kase's, and Bale's chests. Tarron took Willa's hand in his. "It's okay," he whispered.

Scarlet lifted her hands out to her sides and chanted something under her breath. Her eyes widened with surprise and amazement as the students around them panicked, charging in every direction, unsure of where to go. Inside whatever refuge Scarlet provided, the chaos was muffled.

"Yeah, it's okay, Willa," Ana snarled.

Kase stepped up to Ana and reached for her hand. "Leave her alone. Let's just get out of here."

"You are such a wuss!" Ana yelled up to the paper stars. "Our pack needs a real alpha, not some elf-loving, witch-bestie with a pet dragon." She laughed at her insult, but everyone around them took a step back.

Willa bared her teeth.

Ana laughed deliriously. "Like you can do anything about it! Your magic has been suppressed for so long, I'd be surprised if you ever shift."

"Suppressed?" Tarron asked.

Willa seethed at Ana, her inner wolf unable to focus on

words. The supernatural powers she'd kept secret for so long wouldn't be a secret much longer. She balled up her hands into fists, her nails digging into her palms, to tamp down her desire to grab Ana's shoulders and toss her out of their lives.

"Your father should never have assumed the role of alpha," Ana began to ramble. "The next woman in line should have taken over—my mother. Instead, the Kasun pack has weakened, and it'll be up to me to strengthen every member. I'll start with your family." She pointed from Willa to her brother.

Some of the crowd around them had begun to disperse, and Ana's attention wavered. "I'm bored." She turned and walked toward the exit.

Scarlet's arms fell to her sides, and Willa could feel the bubble of magic she'd concealed them in pop.

"Thank you," Willa said.

"Are you okay?" Tarron interrupted. He took her hand in his and she flinched. Willa was bleeding.

Unable to slow her heart rate, Willa knew she had to stop Ana once and for all. She looked Tarron in the eyes and said, "I'll be right back."

Her body broke into a full run after Ana. As she ran, Willa watched Ana heading for the parking lot. The air above her pressed down on her shoulders. She peered up into the sky and found the moon. Only a sliver lit the path ahead of her.

Using the pressure built up in her chest, Willa barked, "Stop!"

And Ana froze in place.

"I'm tired of you." Willa's posture slumped, as she panted for breath.

"Well, that's mutual," Ana slurred. "My family has always deserved to be in control. I have proven myself worthy to be alpha, while you've run away and mated with a garden gnome."

"Your drunken insults won't make you alpha. Walk home and sober up, and leave me and my brother alone from now on," Willa ordered, following her across the football field.

"Oh, I will. And my family will find another way to put you down. I'm surprised that stupid necklace suppressed your magic as long as it did." Ana's eyes darted past Willa, where her friends and their pack gathered. "I was only planning to string your brother along until your birthday at the end of the month. Once I'm officially alpha, I won't need him or your talisman anymore."

Willa's hand flew to her mouth in shock. She'd always known Ana was cold, but her admission had Willa's blood boiling again. "I get doing what you did to me, but how could you even think of using Kase the way you have? You know our birthday is more than a celebration for us."

"Oh, here we go again! Let's sing praises to the perfect alpha and mother who died giving birth to you two. Get over it already!" Ana waved her arms up and down wildly. "She's dead! And there's nothing you can do about it."

Willa swallowed the harsh truth, but the sorrow didn't mix well with her disgust at Ana. Only half of what Ana said was true. It was how she got away with making people feel small. Ana blended the truth with hurtful, debilitating lies.

Willa's mom had been gone a long time, but Willa *could* do something. She didn't have to sit by and let Ana and her family take over. It might not happen right away, but eventually they could manipulate the Court to replace her dad and brothers. They could twist the Kasun reputation until they had to leave town. Fighting her habit of walking away, Willa stepped toward Ana, allowing her supernatural abilities to reach their potential. She felt her shoulder muscles ripple, and she heard Ana's heart begin to race.

"What do you think you can do to me?" Ana asked and took a step back. She broke eye contact and inspected the area around them. They'd moved beyond the athletic fields, and the crowd had followed. "I will be the next alpha, and I plan to make your life a living hell."

"You already do." Willa didn't want to live another day having to answer to Ana, and she knew the only way to remain in control of her fate, as well as protect her pack, would be to take control herself. To shift.

Unsure how to channel the moon's power or the magic inside her, Willa opened up to the wolf calling. She expected the same hindrances she'd felt in the past, but something had changed. The barrier her necklace had created was gone. She supernaturally flexed her strength and hearing, and she felt stronger than ever. Her magic reached up to meet the moonlight, and it shimmered like the stars above her.

Willa heard someone move behind her, and in the same moment Ana rushed them. In her peripheral vision, Willa noticed Tarron's white hair. Her protective instincts took over, and she leapt between them.

Willa's muscles tensed, and her bones cracked. The cool air around her did nothing to soothe the sharp pain erupting at every joint. As her body healed, it broke again, until the rhinestones on her dress flew in the air and the fabric ripped from her body. Her teeth and fingernails grew to points, pushing through gums and skin. Canine teeth brushed against her lips as she snapped protectively, and Willa knew she could rip Ana apart if she wanted. Dark glossy hair covered her body. She'd never felt stronger or more aware. By the time she landed, a black wolf stood guard in front of Tarron.

A growl erupted from Willa, and Ana, still in her human form, bowed her head in submission. Tarron was the first to move, and he hesitantly placed his hand on Willa's neck. She responded by rubbing her head against his hip. Something in the air around her vibrated, and Tarron gasped. As Willa turned her head, a gray and white wolf advanced.

Ana, in her wolf form, stood a few inches shorter, but she'd had more experience controlling her animal nature. Her snarling teeth bit at Willa's neck, but Willa shuffled back and swiped her sharp claw at Ana's face. Ana yelped and retreated, cowering on her belly a few feet away.

Willa looked back to check on Tarron. The pack watched

intently. She let a growl rumble in her chest as she stepped toward Ana. The bark that followed caused Ana to flinch, but she quickly bared her teeth in dissent. Willa prowled closer, and Ana thrust herself under her belly, desperately pawing at anything to gain an advantage. Reacting to the pain, Willa snapped at Ana's neck and flipped her over. The gray and white wolf whimpered in submission.

Tarron rushed to Willa, checking her fur for blood. As he stood, he gritted out, "Ana, I think you should be going."

She left without a word.

Willa walked on all fours to where her dress had landed. She nudged it with her snout in Tarron's direction. She was surprised at the control and understanding she had in her wolf form. Growing up in the pack, she'd heard stories about werewolves who had lost their connection to their human form. She had a good feeling shifting wouldn't be too difficult, just painful and embarrassing. Her dress was ruined.

"Give me a minute," Tarron said before running back into the gym. He waved the crowd back into the dance with him.

Willa watched Ana mope away while she waited. She knew their feud was far from over, but Ana had lost any chance of becoming alpha when Willa released her wolf.

Her ears perked up when she heard the door open. Tarron raced out with a pair of blue running shorts, probably from the locker room, and a black t-shirt with a moon graphic. She cocked her head to the side, wondering if he had another shirt on under his suit jacket. Then, he started to take it off.

Nope. No shirt.

He raised his jacket like a curtain and waved it around. "You can shift behind this and put these on."

Willa knew this was crazy. She'd finally let her wolf out, at homecoming, and now her boyfriend was going to lend her his T-shirt so she could shift back. Her brothers had needed her help with their transitions before, so she was prepared for the change. Willa just hoped Tarron could handle the sounds of her bones breaking and skin tearing without glancing to check on her. She walked over to the brick wall and waited for Tarron to meet her. He lifted the jacket, and Willa yelped at him.

"Fine, I'll close my eyes." He grinned.

Willa thought of her human reflection and stretched her legs in an effort to stand. The shift followed, and the sound of ripping muscles and popping joints made Tarron's face cringe. The change hurt, and Willa struggled to get the T-shirt over her head at first. She slipped the shorts on, then fell into Tarron's jacket and arms.

He didn't pull away.

Someone cleared their throat behind them. Willa pushed up on her toes to look over Tarron's shoulder and saw Scarlet, Bale, and her brother. Scarlet frowned as if repulsed, and Willa knew they'd at least heard her shift. The others had firsthand experience with the process.

"Dad's gonna flip!" Kase exclaimed.

Willa looked down at the watch strapped to Tarron's wrist. It was only a few minutes past ten. "Only if I'm late for curfew." She grinned up at Tarron.

"What do you want to do now?" he asked.

"I want to kiss you."

Tarron leaned down and wrapped his arms around her waist. He nestled his lips against her neck and pressed a trail of kisses up to her lips. Willa's hands slid up his bare chest to his shoulders. She tilted her head back and took his bottom lip between hers. Deepening the kiss, she savored the flavor of cinnamon he left behind.

She pulled back to look at him. "Ask me what else I want?"

"What else do you want?"

"To dance." She winked at him.

EPILOGUE

$\mathcal{F}$riday afternoon, in the school cafeteria, Willa joined Tarron, Bale, and Scarlet at their designated table. Much of the student body buzzed with gossip about the latest *it* couple getting together and the hardest biology test they'd taken. Willa caught a blue bow in her peripheral vision and turned to find Maria sitting with a group of cheerleaders, all donning uniforms for that night's basketball game. Willa smiled as she reached to tug the hem of her top down and remembered she was wearing a comfy tee.

"Do you miss it?" Tarron asked. He noticed the smallest things when it came to her.

Willa rolled her eyes. "Only the bow, but I have a much bigger bow I plan to wear after school."

"I get why you quit the squad, but you're going to miss flying," Bale interjected.

Scarlet nudged him with her shoulder. "You mean you won't give her a lift, Drogon?"

"Sounds fun!" Willa clapped.

Bale scoffed. "You're no dragonrider. You're an alpha. Plus, I don't give rides to just anyone."

Willa smiled to herself as she retrieved her apple and a

protein bar. Things were good. She'd chosen to fight for Tarron, but she'd never imagined it would take giving in to her wolf. What she thought were two worlds warring within her turned out to be one world she was ripping apart by trying to live up to everyone else's expectations.

With her shift came other changes. Her pack learned of the Novaks' betrayal and that Willa could have shifted with the others her age if it hadn't been for the talisman they'd imbued with dark magic. Her openness about her relationship with Tarron had even offered some of the other pack members permission to pursue friendships outside of the pack.

"Hey," Tarron began. "What is your brain up to in there?" He tucked a few strands of hair behind her ear.

She cased the cafeteria one more time before answering, "Just looking for Kase and Elle."

"They'll be here," Scarlet said. "It's not like they can get into any trouble. Everyone is watching them. It's kind of creepy."

"Kase said he's not jumping into anything too fast, so I'm afraid *everyone* is going to be disappointed," Willa informed the group. She'd moved back into the cabin with her dad and Kase, while her brother Tate moved out. Tate explained that her choices helped him to make his own.

Tarron wrapped his arm around her shoulders. "Let's talk about something fun. Like your birthday." He waggled his eyebrows up and down.

"Since it's on a Tuesday, it's not like we can throw a crazy party," Willa said, hoping the others would take the hint that she'd like to keep it low key.

"How about we get coffee, then try our hand at some trick or treating?" Scarlet asked with a wink. Thankfully, her newest bestie had asked what she wanted to do a few days ago.

"That would be hilarious." Bale leaned forward and whispered, "Too bad your costume from homecoming was shredded into ribbons."

Tarron chuckled, and Willa swiftly jabbed him with her

elbow. He rubbed his abs, feigning discomfort. "We could get coffee, and maybe just hang at one of our houses."

"That sounds perfect," Willa agreed, as she nestled into Tarron's side.

Tuesday 5:16 PM

Willa: Is everyone still good for coffee @ 6?

Tarron: Yep

Elle: I'll be a few minutes late

Willa: Are you with the boy version?

The BOY Version: I heard that

Scarlet: I'm already here studying

Bale: Me too

Willa: B, are you studying a book or Scarlet?

Bale: :p

The BOY Version: We'll be there soon

Willa: Great! I may be a few minutes late

Bale: Where's T?

Tarron: studying ;)

Scarlet: Curious, why are we meeting?

Willa: Ha. Ha. Just want to get the Scooby gang together

Tarron: You know, now that Willa's shifted we'll have to recast. Maybe we should let her be Scooby since it's her birthday?

Bale: Not a chance

We hope you enjoyed this story in the Havenwood Falls High series of novellas featuring a variety of supernatural creatures. Read on for an excerpt of *Reawakened* (A Havenwood Falls High Novella) by Morgan Wylie. The series is a collaborative effort by multiple authors. Each book is generally a stand-alone, so you can read them in any order, although some authors have written sequels to their own stories. Please be aware when you choose your next read.

Books by Kallie Ross in the Havenwood Falls universe:

Written in the Stars
A Pack of Lies
Promise the Moon
Defying Gravity

You might also like these books in the Young Adult Havenwood Falls High series:

Somewhere Within by Amy Hale
Bound by Shadows by Cameo Renae
Saving Infiniti by Rose Garcia
Predestined by Valia Lind

Stay up to date at www.HavenwoodFalls.com

ABOUT THE AUTHOR

Writing unique adventures with heart.

Kallie Ross has a passion for writing that has become an adventure in itself. She desires to create unique young adult fiction that incorporates legend, conjecture, fantasy, and conviction.

In addition to loving her life as a writer, Kallie adores being a wife, mother, friend, and teacher. She began her creative journey with books, a blog, a podcast, and lots of caffeine. Ross never imagined her own adventure would be filled with so many wonderful people or words!

KallieRoss.com
Kallie Ross Facebook Page
@KallieRoss Twitter
@KallieRoss Instagram

ACKNOWLEDGMENTS

I want to give a shout out to the amazing Kristie Cook. Her confidence in me as a writer and her dedication to making me better is real friendship! I'm so thankful to have her in my life, and I feel honored to write characters who live in Havenwood Falls. Other friends like Morgan Wylie, Gaby Robbins, and Megan Kennedy inspired me to have fun writing Willa's story, and their support is always a blessing.

Thank you readers! Your enthusiasm for fiction keeps me writing, and your passion for fantasy and the supernatural inspires me.

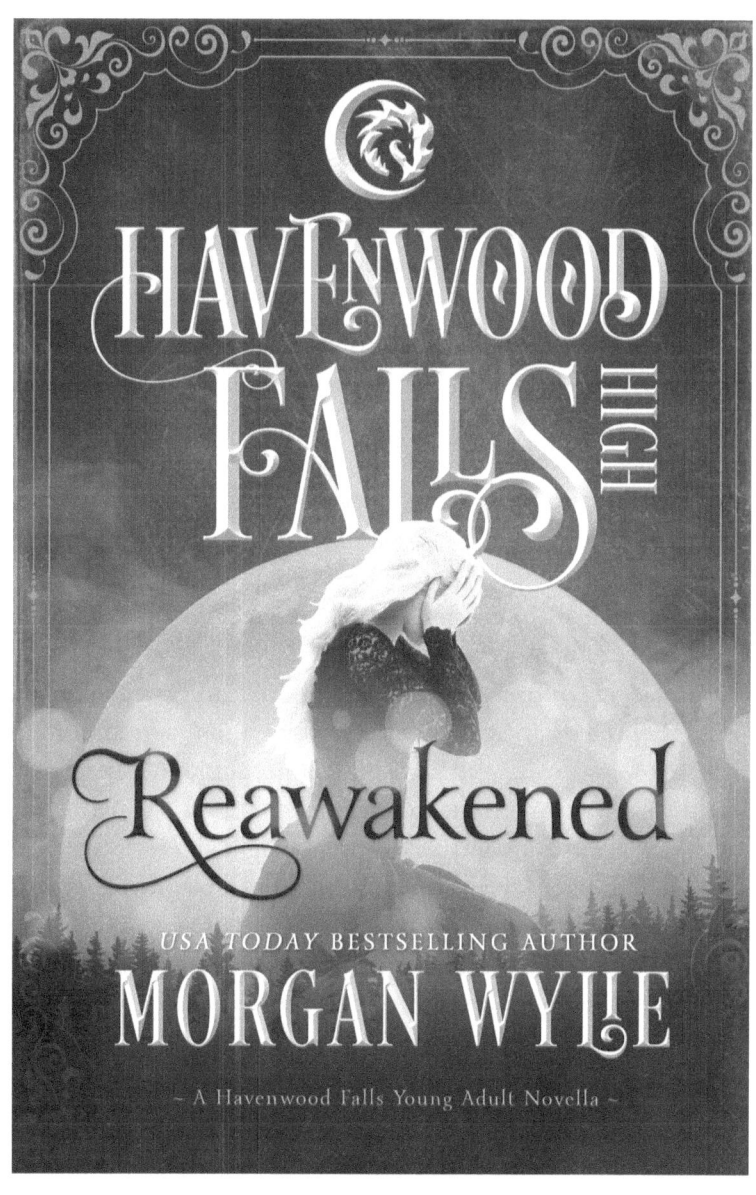

HAVENWOOD FALLS HIGH

Reawakened

USA TODAY BESTSELLING AUTHOR

MORGAN WYLIE

~ A Havenwood Falls Young Adult Novella ~

Reawakened (A Havenwood Falls High Novella) by Morgan Wylie

Like all young witch hunters in Havenwood Falls, seventeen-year-old Macy Blackstone has been spelled to control her killer instincts. When she's reawakened too early, though, her world flips upside down.

Daughter to the Blackstone witch hunters' matriarch, Macy should have known what was coming, but her mother hadn't prepared her. Overwhelmed with the surge of energy from the new moon coupled with a solar eclipse, she's unable to handle the new sensations, and she flees town. To her surprise, she discovers an entire family branch of witch hunters living nearby. Only, the more she gets to know them, the more she learns about their dark intentions for both the witches and the Blackstones of Havenwood Falls.

Gallad Augustine, witch and boyfriend extraordinaire, possesses powerful magic, but Macy took off too soon for him to help her. Now, as her soul mate, his connection to her heart may be the only way for anyone to reach her.

Macy has one moon cycle—twenty-eight days—to uncover the witch hunters' plans and return home before the town's wards wipe her memory permanently and she forgets everything about her family, her home, and her one true love. And if she can't remember them, she won't be able to save them.

REAWAKENED

AN EXCERPT

Most seventeen-year-olds about to enter their senior year of high school enjoyed every last bit of their summer break. Some even went on vacations. Not me—Macy Blackstone, witch hunter. All I wanted to do was forget the title and be normal at least for a day, but apparently that day was not today.

Nearing the end of August in Havenwood Falls, Colorado, the weather had already began to change—not that it ever stayed any particular temperature for long. Up in the mountains especially, fall came earlier than in the lower elevations. The nights grew chilly earlier, and mornings like this one reminded me what I loved about fall.

Cozy in my oversized, chunky cable-knit wrap sweater, I snuggled into the corner of a large outdoor sectional sofa in front of a giant rock fireplace. Stretching out my legging-clad legs, complete with warm Uggs on my feet, I sighed with contentment. I watched the town come to life below me while I slowly sipped from the steaming mug of coffee in my hand. Rays from the sunrise streaked down to touch the edge of our deck, stretching as far as the fire pit and the uncovered section of deck. The reverse would happen just the same again at sunset. Tipping my head up, I closed my eyes, absorbing warmth from the sun's kiss as it crept up my face, inching as far as the roof above would allow it.

"Beautiful, isn't it?" My mom's voice floated from the doorway separating the kitchen from the outside living area.

"It is," I answered, looking back at her. My mom, Lilith Blackstone, was a beautiful woman, appearing in her mid-forties —though she was actually a bit older. For a human, she looked forty-five, but as a hunter, she was still relatively young at seventy-eight years old. Most of the women in my family were hunters—witch hunters to be exact, though we didn't actively hunt witches. My mom was descended from the founding Blackstone family, a strong lineage of witch hunters. She also held a seat on the Court of the Sun and the Moon as the representative and matriarch for our entire family.

"Are you seeing Gallad today?" she asked, moving toward the railing, carrying her own steaming mug.

"I'm supposed to meet him at the vineyard pretty soon, actually." I checked the time on my phone.

Her eyes were on me, watching me, the weight of her assessing stare boring into me. Turning to face her, I couldn't place her expression. Was she upset? She seemed more questioning than anything else.

"Is something wrong, Mom?"

"How are you feeling?" she returned, avoiding my question.

"Um, fine thanks, but don't think I am that easily diverted. What's up?"

Coming over to me, she placed her hand on the back of my neck, now free from my silky blonde locks since I piled them on top of my head in a messy bun that morning. "How is your injury?"

"It's much better since the witches gave us that healing salve to put on it." Reflexively, I touched the back of my neck as well after she pulled away. "There's some scabbing where the stupid tree limb tore my flesh off, but otherwise I think it's good. See?"

I pulled the neck of my sweater down, and tugged my T-shirt back for her to see it.

In a reckless attempt to be normal, I had climbed a tree and tried to jump to an adjacent tree like some damn spider-monkey wannabe. The new tree didn't want to be my friend and wouldn't let me grab hold of it until I had slid down part way, taking my flesh off as I went.

"Your hunter marking looks to be untouched. However, your protection tattoo got a bit roughed up. Did you have Saundra Beaumont look at it like I asked?"

Saundra Beaumont sat on the high council of the Luna Coven, making her one of the most powerful witches in town.

Since I was born, my parents and the Court knew what I would become based on a stupid skin discoloration on the back of my neck in the shape of a cluster of small stars. All hunters were born with it, like a birthmark—or a beacon of doom.

"Yes, Mom. She said it looked fine, and I shouldn't have any issues with the wards within my tattoo. Addie looked at it, too. She said she'd need to touch up a few of the lines but would wait until the skin was fully healed. They both agreed the tattoo held enough magic that it shouldn't be an issue to wait until it was time for the permanent one."

In Havenwood Falls, all the supernatural residents received a tattoo infused with magic. The markings were there for not only our protection, but also for the town's. They protected each individual race, but also helped temper and conceal magic from our human residents, who made up about half of our population. Visitors also had to register with the Court of the Sun and Moon to receive a temporary tattoo for the duration of their stay.

As I grew older, into double digits, the Luna Coven placed a magical, invisible-to-the-eye marking in the shape of a crescent moon with a dragon right below my birthmark. The tattoo was a temporary marking intended to suppress any hunter tendencies until I turned eighteen. According to our traditions as witch hunters, at the age of eighteen we go through a ceremony, committing ourselves to abide by the rules and laws of Havenwood Falls. Hunters can choose for themselves then if they are going to go out on their own, never to return to Havenwood Falls, or become a suppressed member of the Blackstone family and town at large. Good options, right? Normal human high schoolers didn't have to deal with that kind of crap. Choice made and ritual completed, we then receive the permanent tattoo of an adult, thus becoming an official citizen of Havenwood Falls.

"Speaking of which, Macy, I need to speak with you about your upcoming birthday and marking ceremony." A slight edge laced Mom's words, anticipating my reply.

I sighed. This was an old conversation. My eighteenth birthday was coming up the beginning of October.

"Mom, we've talked about this. I still have some time. Can we not talk about it yet? School is starting soon and I want to enjoy the last of summer. Since I can't go anywhere interesting, I want to try to be as normal as possible while I still can." Even I could hear the bitterness and whiny petulance in my tone.

"Macy," she practically growled enough to rival one of the Kasun wolves. The Kasuns were not only the largest werewolf pack in Havenwood Falls, but their alpha, Ric Kasun, was also the town sheriff. "You have put this off for too long. The ceremony will happen, and you need to be prepared. There are things you should know and things to prepare for."

Jumping up from my no-longer-quiet space, I faced her. Then she did something I was not expecting. Moving to the side, she revealed another woman standing behind her in the kitchen, watching the interaction with a frown. Looking from the new arrival back to my mother, I scowled.

"You brought Grandma into this?" Fury pulsed through my veins. I loved my grandmother, and I was normally a reasonable —okay, *somewhat* reasonable—person, but she went behind my back like I needed some kind of intervention.

Eva Blackstone, aka Grandma, was regularly brought in when my mom didn't get her way—at least it looked that way to us kids, my two brothers and myself.

"Now, Macy, be rational. There are many details to attend to and your orientation to complete," Grandma chided from the kitchen, beckoning me inside. Tall, slender, and confident, my grandmother held an air of regality and pride. Her hair had been a fierce blond bob since I could remember, mirroring the same edge in her personality.

"This is my last year of high school, and I'll spend most of it as an official Blackstone hunter. I just want to spend the rest of my summer as an irresponsible teenager. Is that too much to ask?" I huffed and folded my arms across my chest.

"Yes, it is," Grandma said flatly. "You have a responsibility to this family and this town. It is time you owned up to it."

I put my mug in the sink and took several slow drags of air, cooling my growing temper.

"Macy, nothing changes once you are marked. It's all in your head," Grandma added.

I shot a glance toward my mom still standing in the doorway. Her gaze was off in the distance, watching the rising sun or something else farther away, locked in the recesses of her mind. Distracted, she finally felt my stare and looked back to me. I frowned.

"I don't know about that, Grandma," I whispered. My mom definitely had times when she was off, but lately, it had been more obvious. She was hiding something, but I didn't know what.

"Oh that's ridiculous, child. You have until the end of summer and then you will take your place in this town as a Blackstone hunter or . . ."

I spun my head in her direction, mouth open wide. "There's an 'or' in your sentence?"

"Macy, you know the rules of Havenwood Falls. If a witch hunter will not choose to be permanently marked, they cannot remain a resident here," my mother interjected. "And because of the memory wards around the borders, whoever chooses not to stay and follow the laws will forget everything about Havenwood Falls, including their family."

"I know the laws, but I don't need my family threatening me with them either." My heart suddenly felt heavy and sad. I knew they didn't mean to hurt me, but still they did. I grabbed my messenger bag off the counter and moved swiftly through the large, rustic yet modern kitchen-dining-great room toward the front door.

"Where are you going, young lady?" Grandma's voice echoed through the room.

"I'm meeting Gallad at the vineyard, then I have to go into the square to pick up my check at Broastful Brews." I sighed, then schooled my voice to an acceptable tone. "I'm sorry, I just need some space. I'll be back later."

"Let her go, Mom. I'll talk to her again later." My mom's voice reached me before I opened the front door.

I took the shortcut from my house in Havenwood Heights over to Stone Falls Winery without having to head down to the main road. My brothers and I had cut through the fields and forest since we were little, thus wearing down our own path from our main house to our home away from home at the vineyard.

My family had several businesses, including the one I headed to now. Stone Falls Winery had been in my family for generations—since the first hunter, Marie Blackstone, had set up camp. More recently, we added Soothing Sips, a wine-tasting bar in town square, and NamaStays Inn at the Vineyard—a quaint B&B boasting six cabins with picturesque mountain views set amidst the vineyard. My family added them about ten years ago, when we started to see more tourists and visitors to the town.

My father, Reginald "Reggie" Benton Blackstone—the men who married into our family took the Blackstone name—was human and ran the daily operations of the vineyard. Even the extended family was heavily involved with each endeavor, always had been. Grandma's cousin, Great Aunt Letti—Letitia Blackstone, former family matriarch—even oversaw the Yoga in the Vines classes, and she was practically 116 years old! Okay, so she looked like she was in her seventies, but still. Long life ran in the Blackstone family.

Everything about Stone Falls Winery was designed to bring soothing relaxation to your senses, and calm was a necessity for the hunters of my family. The drives and instincts of the witch hunters were strong even with the Luna's magic suppressing the bulk of it. At just the right height, the winery sat above the town providing a view of all of town square. When night blanketed the valley, the town lights and sounds mesmerized even the grumpiest of guests. But when a large moon crested over the tips of the craggy peaks, the sight stopped me in my tracks; I could stare for hours like nothing else mattered. I had memories from when I was small of reaching up, thinking I could touch the tip of the moon because it appeared so close.

Several buildings, modern yet mixed with rustic architecture —similar to our home—were laid out with designed precision. Each was positioned to ensnare the majestic views of snow-capped, jagged mountains.

I maneuvered my way quickly through those buildings, hoping to not get caught by Aunt Letti, lest I be roped into some odd job I was not assigned today. Plus, I already had plans.

"You really shouldn't text and walk at the same time. You're liable to miss something right in front of you." Gallad's voice arrested me. I smiled. Leaning against the back wall of NamaStay's lobby, with one booted foot propped up behind him and sheltered in the shade from the roof line, Gallad was the image of a bad boy in his black leather jacket covering a rock band T-shirt accompanied by gray-washed jeans.

"You really shouldn't wait in the shadows for people. Someone might think you were stalking them." I tried to shake off the small fright with sarcastic wit, but my accelerated heart rate said otherwise. When I looked into his eyes, however, my nerves calmed. His love and concern packaged with his cute signature lopsided grin took my breath away.

"You're right." He pushed off from the wall and moved in close. His cologne wrapped around me, the intoxicating aroma pulling me in close. I loved the way he smelled of pine and spices—it made me feel cozy and safe every time. "I'm sorry. I bet I can make it up to you." His grin turned from innocent to devilish in a matter of seconds as he leaned in to steal a kiss. In that moment, I felt our connection—I was home.

Gallad Augustine, grandson to another Luna Coven High Council member, was a witch prodigy. Remarkably handsome with his windswept dark hair, fair skin, and bright green eyes, he was truly an all-around good guy—though he wore the exterior of a bad boy at times—and he was my boyfriend. Yes, it was unheard of for a witch hunter to date a witch, but stranger things had happened in Havenwood Falls.

I couldn't help but cover my heart with my hand. The beats sped up when he was near—they always did. Those girlish butterflies took flight in my stomach no matter how much I tried to suppress them.

"You definitely have a way of making it up to me," I mumbled in a swoony state. If anyone had told me I would be the type to swoon, I would have laughed in their face. But Gallad could make me swoon pretty much without trying. Grabbing my hand, he laced his fingers in mine and pulled me alongside him as we strolled through the vines of grapes.

"Have you seen any of the Perseids meteor shower? I saw several shooting across the sky last night. It was amazing, Gallad." I couldn't help the awe I heard in my own voice, but they were truly a sight to see.

Gallad's face turned down to me with a smile so big it reached his eyes. "I did. The meteors looked like shooting stars." He looked up as if he could see them already, but the sky still had plenty of color. "I thought of you the whole time, wishing I was lying on the ground somewhere with you, watching the meteors together."

I blushed. The rush of heat ran up my neck and into my face. Squeezing his hand in mine, I changed the subject. "How was your morning?"

He shrugged casually. "Pretty uneventful. You?"

Frowning, I didn't want to talk about my morning. *Way to start a conversation you didn't want to participate in, Macy*, I scolded myself. Too late—he caught my frown.

"What's wrong, Mace?"

"My mom tried to push the marking ceremony on me again." I sighed. "This time she brought my grandmother in on it. That didn't go over too well."

Running my fingers through the tendrils of hair that slipped down from my messy bun, I felt guilty for bringing the topic up. "I'm sorry. I didn't want to drag you into it."

"What are boyfriends for if not to be there when needed?" His cute smile melted my heart and soothed my guilt.

"Thank you," I said sheepishly.

"Hey, how is your back where you were almost skinned alive by a revenge-hungry tree?"

I laughed out loud. "That tree *was* out for revenge, wasn't it?" Shifting my shoulder blades as if testing out my injury for his benefit, I smiled. "It's almost healed."

Gallad kept quiet as we continued walking, but I felt him glance my way several times. I could practically feel the wheels turning in his head.

"Come out with it already, before you burst."

He blew out a gush of air and raked the fingers of his free hand through the hair sliding down into his eyes. "I know you don't need me to add to it, but you know how important your permanent tattoo is. I'm sure Cousin Addie would do it as soon as your skin fully heals."

"She would, and she offered." Slowly, I brought air in through my nose as I calmed my inner nerves. The idea of being permanently chained left me raw, no matter how much I loved my town. I mean, I knew I'd be able to leave town someday. Since I was little, I always wanted to step outside the boundaries of Havenwood Falls—even just for one day, to see what else was out there, how other people lived, what it might be like to live in a normal town. Just once. I wanted to travel!

Mom and Dad left often for short business meetings and quick getaways, but they had never taken me or my younger brother, Brice. They always returned within the necessary twenty-eight-day moon cycle. In fact, they had never risked more than two weeks. As a human, my older brother Brock got to go with them a couple times, and even had tried attending college outside of town, but he didn't have much desire, it seemed, to travel. I would do anything to leave for college, but apparently it wasn't in my cards—or so I'd been told—because I was marked as a hunter. Literally. Alas, I would have to wait a little while longer. Until then, I would do what I could to pretend I was a normal seventeen-year-old, headed into her senior year at Havenwood Falls High.

"I'm just not ready yet."

"I won't push you, Mace. But I have plans for us, you and me, and don't want anything to get in the way of them." Gallad turned a smile on me that rivaled a rogue pirate.

My heart thumped up into my throat. All salivary glands stopped working at once, drying out my mouth. And those damn butterflies took flight so fast, they almost knocked me off my feet. Words. I couldn't find words.

Purchase Reawakened at your favorite book retailer.